Paragon

Fall of Man

Zane Palmer

Paragon

Fall of Man

by

Zane Palmer

Paragon Fall of Man
© 2020 Zane Palmer

Chapter Information

Chapter One

A SOUND OF THUNDER WOKE SCOTT CARTER FROM HIS SLEEP. ON any given morning he would hear the ring of his phone as it buzzed in alarm. His room was dark. Outside the world was growing darker. lightning provided a glimpse of his small apartment loft. His bed was warm, having shared it that night with his girlfriend Daphne. Her arm draped across his waist as he gently broke away from her comfort. Her blonde hair broke the darkness of the night as she remained dormant. Thunder rumbled outside as Scott made his way into his tiny bathroom. Still clutching the doorknob, Scott's free hand traced the wall. Ever since he was a kid he did this. Caressing the drywall his fingertips met the light switch. Expectations flat-lined in an instant.

The room remained dark as the sound of ventilation roared to life. Swift as ever, Scott's hand slapped the switch again. Silence. The echo of thunder replaced the static. Scott maneuvered the adjacent switch on the wall. Brightness blinded him. His reflection in the mirror met up with him through blinking blue eyes. His exhausted mirror image caught up with him in a stare. Dark hair fell over his brow. His slender figure hunched over the limited sink. Sleep hung from the corners of his eyes. This stare lasted longer than most would. Scott was humble about his looks, he spent time in the mirror like this giving himself motivation. Work loomed in the distance of his thoughts.

Scott Carter had grown up in a small household in a small Oklahoma town. Graduation from high school had offered him little interest in pursuing further education. Instead he opted out for life living in the city, with his older brother. The two of them worked their way into many jobs. Scott found himself growing within the ranks of Paragon Car Wash, owned by Mr. Donald C. Webb. Scott first met Mr. Webb in his early twenties while working for a competitor. The older man took a liking to Scott, and when the opportunity struck, they both benefited. Going to work for Paragon Car Wash and Mr. Webb meant that Scott could break free from his brother's support. His life began to pick up as Scott was able to get a car and apartment of his own. When Scott was twenty-two years old he moved into Sunset Plaza, settling with a small loft on the third floor. It was quaint and more than enough space for the young man, at five hundred fifty square feet. Sunset plaza got by for sixteen years under the management of The Rodrigues Family. They treated all their tenants as family, and their three boys were no exception. Sunset plaza was their playground, and Scott was someone they enjoyed to have around. Six years and two couches later, Scott has been content with his life.

Lightning danced the silhouette of the bathroom window. Scott did his business and rinsed his hands in a hurry. The early hour meant that he could return to his bed, and to the peace of sleep. Fond memories of adolescence filled his mind as he turned the copper faucet knobs. Memories of his father rescuing him from a stubborn faucet in youth.

Scott was too young to understand their function. Something that crossed his mind during nightly breaks like these. His father would walk him back to bed, or sometimes he'd sleep in his parents' room. Rain was now knocking on his window as memory guided Scott back to his bedroom. Daphne's blonde hair still shining through. Warm blankets embraced him as his arm scooped her close. Scott's world faded in the rain, as he drifted back to sleep.

By the time Scott's alarm interrupted his dreams he was alone. Emptiness shared his bed as thoughts took hold of him. Snatching the phone up from the nightstand, Scott wasted no time standing. His morning routine was quick, as work was around the corner. outside the storm kept pace. A knock on Scott's door interrupted the young man.

Phone in hand, Scott made his way to the door. He peeked through the peephole at an older man standing in the hallway. It was his apartment superintendent, Tiago Rodrigues.

Scott opened the door for Tiago.

"Ola! bom dia, Scott" Tiago said in a low voice.

He kept his hair short and his mustache pristine on his upper lip. His age was in his eyes, and his forehead had wrinkled from stress. His stature meant he looked up to Scott, but his dominance was intact. Their relationship was always fair, although they had to maintain business.

"Good morning," Scott replied.

Tiago shifted where he stood. "Scott," he started. "I need to know when you plan on paying me rent for this month?" He began to dig in his pocket. A small piece of paper now in his hand and extended out for

Scott. He unfolded it and recognized his handwriting. Before Scott could speak Tiago continued, "You signed this paper for me Scott. I didn't ask for it but you signed it at the beginning of the month when you said you didn't have your rent money." Scott looked away from the paper and met the ready gaze of Tiago. "It's been almost three weeks now," Tiago declared. Scott shifted slightly.

Even in the hallway thunder could be heard. Scott's smile turned into words as he spoke, "I know-I'm sorry." Scott apologized. "Trust me Mr. Rodrigues, I'll have it in a few days," Scott said, folding the paper in his hand. Tiago leaned in, arching an eyebrow and asked, "what is a few days?" Scott's phone broke the conversation with the sounds of alarm. He ignored it and slid his phone back inside his pocket. "Friday," Scott sighed, "I'll have rent ready then." Tiago's demeanor was more calm as he cracked a smile. Another alarm chimed in on Scott's phone. He pulled it out to check the screen as Tiago said something unnoticed. There was a weather update going off for Scott to deactivate.

Tiago was growing impatient as Scott slid his phone back inside his pocket. "Sorry," Scott said apologetically. "I'm used to it with three boys at home. Drives their mother nuts." Tiago laughed. The two of them shared a laugh as Scott's mind lingered back to work. His laugh lost its energy. Tiago picked up on this and began to ask the younger man about it. "How is work going, eh? My wife is still thankful you got Javier out of the house." Tiago smirked. Scott returned a smile and nodded. "He's great Mr. Rodrigues," Scott assured him. Tiago nodded in unison. "I don't want to be rude, but I was actually in the middle of getting ready for work when you came by," Scott confessed. Tiago took a firm stance, still smiling. "My apologies Scott," he said dismissing himself.

After Mr. Rodrigues had left, Scott rushed to get dressed and start his day. He put on his work uniform, a red button up shirt with two patches on it. One patch bore his name and title; Scott Carter, Assistant Manager. The other patch had his company logo, resting on his heart. His khaki pants stained with various soap colors and grime.

Scott ran through the rain and made his way to his car. The interior had a unique smell to it. He is known to his friends as someone who enjoyed smoking marijuana more than most people. Even before his home state and others had legalized the recreational use of the plant. However, Scott's habit was unhealthy. As he would often smoke in his car during work hours and during breaks. He cared for his work and was confident in his own performance and actions. In his mind his actions were justified regardless of the risk it presented him. As Scott started the engine to idle, rain began to fall on his windshield. The radio came on as it always did when the car started up. The news could be heard over the speakers as Scott dug in his pocket to collect his things. He sat his phone in the cup holder of the center console as the woman on the radio described the forecast for the day.

Scott's lighter flicked to life in his hand, as his loaded bowl filled the small interior with its rich aroma. Smoke filled his lungs as a calming state of mind began to wash over him. *It's time to hit the road before I'm late,* he thought. The reverse lights shined in the rain as he pulled out from a parked position. His mind was on one thing, breakfast.

A faint beeping sound came on in his car telling him it was time to get gas. Rock music entertained him as he found his way to a gas station.

He ran inside the store as cold rain pelted him. It was colder than usual for that time of year. Scott's red shirt soaked by the time he got inside the store. The clerk was towards the back, stocking bagged chips and snacks. Scott grabbed a canned coffee energy drink and made his way over to the front counter. The clerk took a minute to notice that Scott was standing there waiting. The young man stood up and removed headphones from his ears as he approached Scott. "Good Morning, bud," the young man said. Scott was smaller than the man and looked up to him behind the counter. "Can I get you anything else?" the clerk asked as his register beeped at the sound of Scott's coffee scanning.

Scott looked out the front doors of the store. The rain was coming down now. Harder than it had been all morning. He couldn't make out the number for the gas pump he had pulled up to. The clerk, seeing all this had picked up on what was happening and asked, "how much gas would you like?" Scott looked back over to the man who was smiling and Scott replied, "yeah, I guess I'm the only car. Can I get ten dollars on the pump out there?" the clerk hit some buttons on his register. "Will that be all?" He asked. Scott reached for his wallet and asked for two chocolate doughnuts from the counter. The clerk leaned down to grab those as he smiled again. "I gotta say, man, I like your cologne," the clerk said as he bagged the doughnuts. Scott thought to himself and remembered that he did not apply any cologne that morning. He was confused until he remembered his recent smoke. "Thanks, it's natural,"

Scott said. He paid the clerk and then braved the cold rain back to his car.

After he finished pumping his gas, Scott opened the trunk of his car. In it, he kept spare clothes for work. The car wash was the type of place where you had to adapt and plan. It was common for Scott's feet to get wet at the beginning of his shift. Scott grabbed a jacket from the trunk and put it over his wet shirt. He had backup shirts at work and didn't want to commit to changing his clothes in a parking lot. The jacket was warm and dry as he got back into his car and fired it up. The sound of the rain on his windshield drowned out the radio as he drove off.

Lightning flashed in the sky as the wind picked up. The lights to the car wash were on, yet the doors to the long tunnel building were closed. His manager was the only one working. Scott cracked the windows of his car to let some of the smell out as he got closer to the parking lot. His car bounced over the speed bump in the entrance as Scott made his way across the empty lot. Inside the building, Scott could see that his manager was on the computer at the desk. The same place he had been the day before as Scott went home.

His manager Ben Miller was a nice guy. He was in his early thirties with the same build as Scott. Ben had light blonde hair with a short brown beard. His glasses rested on his nose as he buried all thought and action into his computer. Ben had a particular management style. He would spend all his time passing assignments down to his staff through Scott. This created a lot of distance between him and the crew at Paragon car wash.

"You're late," Ben said without looking up from his computer.

Scott sat his canned coffee and doughnuts down and went to the bathroom. "Good morning," Scott said as he picked out one of his shirts from the rack. After changing into something dry Scott came out to see Ben putting on rain boots. *Ben never gets his hands dirty,* Scott thought. Ben emptied his pockets and pulled open the door, leading to the car wash tunnel. "Are we doing the pit together?" Scott asked, trying to sound interested. "Yep," Ben replied without enthusiasm.

The two men stepped out into the car wash tunnel together. It had a certain smell of soap and mold, and the lights gave it a gloomy feeling you can expect on a rainy day. They made their way to the back room. They kept the equipment and tools back there. Each man grabbed a shovel and a bucket. After returning to the tunnel Ben pulled back a grate covering the pit below the track. Scott put on rubber gloves and climbed down into the pit.

Down in the pit, the smells are worse than you can imagine. A combination of mold and manure that's sat out in the sun. The number of cars that get washed every day depends. Cleaning the pit is a task that doesn't get done unless it's a rainy day. Scott and the crew can't close down the business to get the pit cleaned. It's a job that requires hours of scooping mud and sludge. Thousands of cars may pass through before it ever gets touched.

Scott and Ben worked together for about half an hour before any casual jokes were cracked. They had something of a strained relationship. Ben's approach to management often left more to be desired from Scott. Around the time of the grand opening it became clear to Scott that Ben was not going to fill any mentor roles.

The past two years between them had been a descent into this point that the two of them talked only about work. They kept to themselves otherwise. Ben worked hard, and knew what he was talking about. Instead of working in the tunnel with his employees, He preferred to handle computer work.

Scott's shovel was heavy with mud as he dumped it into his bucket. It was a long process because a five-gallon bucket can fill quickly down there. The pit itself slopes on one side, meeting the ground about four feet under the surface. There is a gap at the bottom of the slope where water flows to keep the pit circulating. Once their bucket was full they would carry it out to the dumpster to empty.

A few hours went by and the two men finished scooping the pit to their liking. Ben climbed out first and helped Scott out. They walked to the dumpster holding their buckets. Scott dumped his mud bucket first as the cold rain continued to pour. The sky was the darkest it had been all day. Ben dumped his bucket out as the wind began to pick up. The lids to the dumpster flew open and the door to the building swung in the wind. "Let's go!" Scott shouted to Ben through pouring rain. Back inside the two of them took turns changing into dry clothes. Ben went first. Scott couldn't help but find it funny that Ben's clothes always look so much cleaner and fresher. About a year ago Ben had married a lovely young woman named Kelly.

Scott changed his clothes and washed mud from his hands. his arms were black from the dirt. He knew he would not have to work much longer with Ben. Thunder rumbled. The lights in the bathroom flashed. Ben was in the office outside making noise.

Scott's phone chimed with the sound of another flood warning. Ben knocked on the door. "Hey, what sounds good for lunch?" Ben asked.

The door swung open and Scott turned off the light as he stepped out. We never eat lunch together, he thought. Scott looked at Ben for a second and then replied, "lets get Mexican food." Ben nodded and grabbed his keys. "Okay, the weathers not getting better so I'm going to a good place I know," Ben explained. "Javier will be here soon so have him do the windows," Ben closed the door behind himself and ran to his car.

a few minutes later Scott decided he would smoke. He kept a secret stash near the back doors in the equipment room. The spot was at the right angle to stay off camera. The equipment room was loud and smelled fruity thanks to the soaps. Scott was confident it was a good hiding spot. Working with Ben worried him a little bit, but they wouldn't spend much more time together. Scott loaded his little pipe and began to take hits. His mind felt more at ease and the smoke rolled out the back door into the pouring rain.

Scott's phone began to ring. Ben was calling. Scott looked around to make sure Ben wasn't watching him. Panic filled his thoughts. Scott sounded nervous as he answered the call, "Hello?" The other end was all background noise between Ben's radio and the sound of rain. "Scott? What are you doing?" Ben asked. *He knows,* Scott thought.

He put his pipe away as if he was being watched. "I'm in the back room," Scott confessed. "Oh great, could you clean the hydro-minders while you're back there?" Ben demanded. "So anyway, you never said what you want from the restaurant?" Ben asked under the sound of thunder. Relieved, Scott told Ben his order and ended the phone call. He pulled his pipe out and turned around to see Javier standing behind him smiling. "You got any more of that?" The young man asked.

Chapter Two

JAVIER RODRIGUES GREW UP IN SUNSET PLAZA. HIS FATHER TIAGO, took over superintendent duties when Javier was still a young boy. Most of his earliest memories came from Sunset Plaza. His mother and father worked hard to provide for him and his two younger brothers, David and Alvin. When Javier was old enough to pick up a broom or grab a screwdriver his father enlisted his help. During the school year Javier was expected to work with his father on weekends. His mother was a nurse. She spent most of Javier's childhood working long shifts, unable to look after her boys. This duty also fell on Javier's shoulders.

Javier was five years older than his brother David.

David was tall for a fourteen year old, with a skinny figure. His curly long dark hair was always a mess. Then there was Alvin, or Al as his family called him. Al was obsessed with his appearance and impressing girls in his fifth grade class.

Out of the three boys Javier was the most handsome. He had a muscular figure and stood taller than his father. His family always told him how much he took after his mother for her looks. Once he was finished with school, Javier planned to leave home. Life had other plans and he didn't get to go to college like he wanted. His time working at Paragon car wash with Scott had been good for him. Not only did it provide extra income to help his family, Javier had an escape from Sunset Plaza. They were nine years apart in age, but Javier always felt like Scott treated him as an adult and equal. Scott would often come into work smelling like smoke. Sometimes late at night Javier could pick up the soothing aroma of marijuana. Most often on nights cool enough to leave the windows open. It wasn't until he worked with Scott that he learned it was coming from his apartment.

Today was a good day for Javier to smoke, after his father spent the morning drinking and rounding up late rent. His only worry was on his brothers getting home from school safe in the bad weather. Javier's car struggled to keep up with the pounding rain as lightning lit his path. His little car parked next to Scott's as he slammed the door, looking down at the ground as the rain blinded his view. Inside, the tunnel was empty. The air stunk worse than usual. He knew that the pit had been cleaned. *I bet they have you shovel the back hole,* he told himself on his way to the back room. The back hole is what they called the second, smaller pit in the back room. It's a hole big enough for one person, and several buckets of foul sludge.

The back room had a breeze and Javier could hear the sound of rain as if he were outside. The back door was open and he found Scott standing in the off camera spot. Scott turned around startled as he saw Javier. "You got any more of that?" Javier asked with a smirk. He told himself he needed this. "Man! you scared me half to death," Scott quipped.

The timing was perfect as lightning struck outside. Thunder echoed overhead. Javier stared out at the menacing storm. Scott's pipe was now loaded and he extended it out to Javier. The two of them smoked together and then hid the evidence. Scott used the bathroom to wash his face and his hands. Javier sat in the office chair and checked the next week's schedule. Today was Tuesday and he would not get a day off for another six days. *Thanks Ben,* He thought. Javier liked Ben, They didn't talk much but he was young and managed a business. Something Javier wanted to work towards. Not to mention Kelly, Ben's wife. It was wrong for Javier to have attraction towards his bosses' wife. Kelly was very active in the car wash community. She helped with events and charities. Her short red hair always fell in her face and Javier longed to be the one to brush it out of her eyes.

Scott came out of the bathroom wearing fresh clothes. As he finished his shirt buttons Ben's headlights appeared in the parking lot. "Okay, Ben's back." Scott pointed out. Javier stood up from the office chair. Ben didn't like it when the employees were in the office and not productive. "Hey so you gotta do the windows today, Ben wanted me to tell you." Scott remembered. *Thanks Scott,* Javier thought, although he was relieved to have something to do. After all, he had been at work half an hour and all he had done was smoke in the back room. Panic hit him, *What if Ben suspects we're high?* his mind teased. Javier rushed by Scott and got into the restroom before Ben made it inside the office.

Ben pushed through the office door as Scott sat reading the schedule. "I've never seen rain like this," Ben said shaking his wet hair. The bag of food in his hands had become soggy. "We're going to close early," Ben teased. Scott took the bag of food from his hands. "Oh yeah?" Scott asked in a cheerful tone. Outside the sky was completely dark. Rain fell like sand in an hourglass. Scott and Ben's phones interrupted the moment, as alarms blared in unison. Ben looked down at the alarm and his eyes got wide. "Or we could end up being stuck here." Ben sighed. *Flash flood warning in effect in your area. Thunderstorms in effect in your area. Wind advisory in your area,* Scrolled across their handheld screens.

The bathroom door swung open. Javier came out as if unaware of the tension. "Bathrooms clean." He declared, looking at the two older men. Thunder rumbled in the distant sky. It sounded like it was right on top of them and didn't let up. Lightning flashed outside and the power went out. Their phones lit the small office as ringtones destroyed all silence. Scott and Ben stepped out of the room to answer their phones, leaving Javier alone. He was sitting with his phone out. Group chatting with his brothers.

Javier did what he could to calm the boys down. Their school bus should have dropped them off at home by now. Javier began to worry as David messaged him saying his bus wasn't there. Al was stuck in the school cafeteria until more buses could arrive. Weather like this was common in the Midwest, but the boys were inexperienced. Scott came back inside from his phone call. Ben was still pacing outside the office. Javier stood up and grabbed his keys. "I gotta go home and get my brothers," he told Scott. The door opened behind them and Ben stepped in. The office was dark except for their phone lights. Scott and Ben convinced Javier that it was a bad time to risk the weather. His brothers were keeping him updated, and their father Tiago was home waiting for them.

The storm raged on. They ate the food Ben had picked up, and played music over their phones. An hour passed and both David and Al had made it to Sunset Plaza. Another hour went by as the three men sat in the dark. Visibility was low, and the streets outside were dark and void of traffic. The wind howled as the power flashed to life. Standing at the door of the car wash was a figure. Rain showered them, concealing their identity. Scott and Ben jumped up as Javier dropped his phone. As fast as the electricity kicked on it was out. Lightning danced across the black sky. *Someone's outside in all this?* Javier questioned. Scott and Ben were already in the tunnel making their way to the door as Javier stood. He stepped out into the tunnel as Scott wrapped his jacket around a blonde woman almost half his size. He embraced her.

Daphne Williams explained how she left work and due to low visibility decided to stop at Paragon. Scott introduced Daphne to Ben. Javier checked his newly cracked phone. Scott and Daphne went to the bathroom so she could change her clothes. Javier and Ben took that time to check the back door. Daphne Had worn Scott's shirts plenty of times, but never his work shirts. They had the unique car wash smell.

Once she was dry and warm, she pulled Scott close. "This weather is scary, are we heading home soon?" She questioned. Scott leaned back from her, to look in her eyes. "Ben thinks we should ride the storm out here, I can't just leave." Scott answered. His eyes found comfort in her gaze. She smiled softly, "well, Baby," she said in a tone that struck Scott to his core. He knew what it meant, where the conversation was going.

"You've said it several times that this isn't a career to you, it's a job. You don't have to stick around here because Ben tells you to." she said in an unforgiving tone. Scott rolled his eyes and began his defense, "Well I'm supposed to be here for another hour. That's the mindset I came in with. Ben was going to let us go early but the storm was so strong we all decided to stay together. We can go home when you want to." Scott and Daphne had slipped out of each other's embrace.

Daphne frowned, "I don't want to keep you from your friends." she said. Scott rolled his eyes, Daphne had seen that several times before. "Why do you have to do that?" she asked. He softened his composure, and reached out for her hand. She reached back. "I'm sorry," Scott started. "We're doing this in the car wash bathroom. Let's drop this and go home soon, does that sound good?" Scott looked down at her, and Daphne nodded. "Yeah, That sounds fine."

Ben and Javier walked through the back room. Javier wanted to ask Ben a question about the equipment they had. Something caught Ben's attention and he walked over to investigate. "Hey, Javier. Come tell me what this looks like to you?" Ben shouted.

Javier had an idea what it might be, but he didn't want to think about that. He knelt down beside Ben, it was dark. *How did he see this?* Javier began to wonder. Ben used his phone as a flashlight. There was nothing in front of them. *What am I looking at?* Javier continued to wonder. Ben put his palm down on the concrete. "you see the corrosion on the ground. From the water in the pressure gun?" Ben asked, trying not to sound nervous or angry. Javier looked at the rusty colored concrete. The surface was rough as Ben rubbed his hand across it. Javier apologized, "okay-sorry." Ben sighed and stood. "I gotta turn it all the way off, huh?" Javier asked. Ben shook his head to confirm.

Javier was still crouched and rubbed the ground with his own palm. He hadn't considered water doing that. Ben looked down at the younger man, "you see, we use city water in the pressure gun. It's not like the soft water we filter for the cars. It's more damaging to surfaces." Javier nodded and stood up beside Ben.

They walked together to the back door. The wind outside was ferocious. The back door stood strong, as Ben pressed his palms against its metal. Javier turned around to look at the entrance, which was too dark to see. "Javier, what's this?" Ben's voice was more alarmed than before. *What's he gonna say this time?* Javier's eyes rolled. He turned around to see Ben holding a pipe and bag of cannabis.

Ben Miller's parents raised him to believe in God and to respect others around him. When he was eighteen he took a job with his father. The job required them to work their neighbors' land as a ranch hand. He did that for several years with his father, until one day he decided it was enough. In fact, he was sick of the lack of available women. The rancher had no daughters. That's about the only place he had the time to meet a woman, as much as he worked. Once he arrived in the city he found work in a parts warehouse. His eyes fixed on a young woman in sales. She was a young redhead with nice curves. Her outfits alone could close a sale. Ben charmed her, and took her on a date. Her name was Kelly Brown. Her father, Mike Brown, employed the both of them at Brown Cars, LLC.

When old Mike found out one of his parts employees was dating his daughter, he fired Ben. Within a year's time, Ben was like a son to Mike. Regret overtook Mike and he tried to make it right and rehire Ben.

Yet, Ben declined out of pride. Kelly had a former roommate, Dana, daughter of car wash tycoon Donald C. Webb.

Dana arranged for Ben to have dinner with her father. When he arrived, Ben felt severely under-dressed. The restaurant staff knew he was too, as they insisted on him wearing the house jacket.

Donald C. Webb was considerably late to the meeting. As he sat down a waiter approached. Ben had been unattended to as he waited. Webb started both men off with tequila shots. By the end of the night, Donald had Ben in his web. He lured him in with promises of many stores under his management. His salary would be based on the success of these stores and his crew. Ben started immediately. Three years later and Ben is still in the same position he was when he started. One store under his command. With three guys as his crew.

The storm was picking up. The doors of Paragon Car Wash stood strong. Ben sat in his office chair, with Scott and Javier facing him. His face showed disappointment. Their eyes were on the ground. Ben looked at each of them and then sighed. "Look guys. I know you smoke, we all do. Just don't do it at work on company time. Got it?" Ben held his eyes on Scott as both his employees looked up in shock. "Wait, did you say you smoke?" Javier asked before Scott could. Ben nodded. "Yeah, everyone smokes back where I grew up." Scott found himself surprised by the revelation. Ben was someone Scott thought would never touch the stuff. Ben chuckled and told Scott to take his stuff with him when he goes home.

The screeching of metal echoed through the small facilities as Daphne charged in. "There's chunks of the roof coming off out there!"

She shouted as Scott put his arms around her. She trembled in his arms as Javier ran to the door. "Help me get this door shut!" he barked. Ben threw himself up against the door with Javier. Ben pushed while Javier managed to turn the lock, securing them inside.

Scott began moving Daphne to the safe room. He grabbed his keys from his pocket and fumbled in the dark with the lock. "Good idea," Ben said as he motioned Javier to go in first. Once the four of them were inside they locked the door behind them. "This safe room isn't limited to protecting money. The wall's reinforcements are designed to be tornado proof." Ben told the group seeking recognition of his own design input. "Well, Baby," Daphne said, turning to Scott. "I don't think we're leaving anytime soon. I'm going to get comfortable." Scott put his arms around her and held her close, "That sounds fine." he replied. Javier propped himself in a corner and Ben laid flat on the floor checking his phone for word from Kelly. No signal.

Chapter Three

MORNING CAME WITH NO WARNING. THE STEADY THUNDER throughout the night had been enough to put everyone's mind on edge. Javier remained sleepless. Ben was the first to wake up, followed by Daphne and Scott. They could still hear the sound of rain, only this time it was much closer. Scott and Ben pulled the door open. It bent into the frame in one of the top corners but after a few attempts they broke free.

Javier ran out past them. He let out an agonizing screech as he ran to his car, which was now inside the car wash. The exterior wall was completely destroyed where the vehicle had entered. Rain fell inside the building as Javier stood soaked in mourning for his car.

Ben looked around analyzing the situation. He looked at Daphne and Scott who were whispering to themselves. "Guys," Javier broke the silence. "I'm ready to go home." Ben grabbed his car keys and pressed his lock button. A beep chimed through the rain. Daphne and Scott had the same idea but Scott's car was gone. Daphne's car was now at the opposite end of the parking lot, but in good condition.

"My priority is my wife right now," Ben said. "She spent the night alone in our house with only our dog to protect her. But all this damage will still be here when the storm settles." Ben was already making his way to the door at this point. Javier watched him go and then made his way over to Scott and Daphne. "So, I can get a ride, right?" he asked, rubbing his wet sleeve. Daphne smiled at him and nodded, "Of course, man." Together the three of them braved the rain and managed to drive off in Daphne's car. Ben's tail lights faded in the distance.

Sunset Plaza remained untouched during the night. Daphne's driving got them there in reasonable time. The roads had cars abandoned and no electricity to light the winding path. The sky was darker than it had been the day before. Scott couldn't help but worry for Javier. His brothers meant so much to him. Scott began to think about his own brother, and his parents. *Were they okay in all this? Were they even experiencing bad weather?* They only lived an hour away after all.

Javier slammed his door and ran inside the building. Scott and Daphne sat alone in the car. Her eyes were on his smile, although he seemed to be putting it on for her. Scott grabbed her hand and kissed it, as if he knew she saw through him. Daphne leaned in for a kiss. Scott's lips met hers. His stubble tickled her nose but she had grown to like it. As they looked into each other's eyes the sky lit up, for the first time. The two of them sat in awe as bright streaks rippled across the sky in their direction.

When Javier got home, he found his family asleep together on the sofa. All three of them, wrapped in each other's arms. Tiago in the middle, with Al on his right and David on his left.

Tiago opened his eyes and saw his oldest son smiling in the doorway. Loud explosions outside transcended the thunder, rocking the building of Sunset Plaza. The windows were blown out during the noise, throwing Javier backwards into the hall.

When the young man opened his eyes the world was a blur. His head pounded in pain as thoughts formed. Once his head felt steadied Javier sat up and looked around. Even in the dark he recognized the familiar scene of his family home. *What's going on?* He wondered. the wind outside howled through the hole in the wall where the window had been. Suddenly there was a loud noise coming from inside his apartment. He couldn't make out the sound but one thing was certain, it was approaching him. Out of the darkness came a bright light. Javier's eyes met the light, blinding him. Before he could blink again a hand was on him. The hand clutched his shirt and in one motion snatched the young man from the ground. Javier was on his feet now, still feeling weak. The light shined bright on Javier as it shifted back to its possessor. Tiago's face Cast its shadow on the ceiling as he placed his free hand on his son's shoulder. "Pop, what happened?" Javier asked in relief. His voice was soft and his throat felt dry. Tiago handed a second flashlight to his son and turned to pick up a bag from the floor. Tiago threw the bag over his shoulder as he spoke, "We're going for your mother Javi, this storm is dangerous". His voice was low but full of emotion Javier had rarely heard from his father. Tiago continued, "Some tenants were running through the halls earlier. They kept yelling about something crashing outside."

Before Javier could speak, a loud thud came from the darkness behind them. Tiago turned to shine his light on his youngest son, Al. The young boy had a scared look on his face as he turned his eyes from the light. "Dad!" Al screamed out. Tiago laughed as he aimed his flashlight to the ground at his son's feet. The door behind Javier swung open and

David emerged from the darkness. Javier's head still hurt but he was at peace knowing his family was unharmed. "I got the bags in the van downstairs, I tried to see the damage," David bragged, soaked from rain. Damage? Javier's mind raced. He had heard something the night before while everyone else slept in the safe room. He assumed it was a tornado that put his car through the wall of Paragon car wash. It must have been. Javier was surprised none of the others woke from the noise. Then again there was Scott's snoring and the rain to deal with. perhaps they had missed something at Paragon.

Thunder boomed above Sunset Plaza pulling Javier out of thought. He was alone, in his bedroom shoving all the clothes he could fit into a bag. His family had moved the last of their things into the van downstairs. Javier dug in the back of his closet and pulled out a small box. There was some weight to the box as Javier removed the lid. Inside was an envelope and an instant camera. He put the camera in his backpack. Javier smiled as he opened the envelope. Pictures of him and his brothers were inside, something to comfort his mother at the hospital. He placed the envelope in his bag with the camera then stood up. Flashlight in hand, Javier ran to the front door of the small apartment. His head no longer hurt, but his heart was Racing. Something inside kept pulling him back to Paragon car wash. The halls of Sunset Plaza were vacant as Javier ran to meet up with his family. The van was barely visible in the rain. It had been completely dark for over twenty four hours now as storms raged on. Javier jumped into the backseat of the vehicle and pulled the door shut behind him. Al was in the back with him, looking out the window at something. "You can't see anything from here," he cried. David who was in the front with their father turned to look back at his sibling. "Calm down Al, you're going to see plenty of it once we get moving!" he barked in response. Javier put his seat-belt on as the family vehicle pulled out into the unknown. The wind was strong and rocked the van as it made its way into the empty street. "Get ready Al!" David cheered. Al sat forward with excitement, as Javier's interest grew. *What is happening?* he thought as the van turned a corner.

A block away from Sunset Plaza there it was, crashed in the street, a satellite. Fire danced around the debris despite the onslaught of rain. Al and David looked on in amazement, but Javier felt the hairs on his neck stand. *What in the world is going on?* Javier thought to himself as they made their way to the hospital. He let out a deep breath as new thoughts filled his head. *Mom, We're coming for you.* He reminded himself as he closed his eyes. Finally he could relax a little.

Scott and Daphne wasted no time clearing out Scott's apartment. They were the only ones running inside as everyone else panicked to leave. Daphne scrambled to get her phone to work but it was no use. Scott's bag was packed and ready in an instant. Daphne collected her things while he ran into the halls to check what was happening. Most of the tenants had left and the halls were now silent. At the end of the hall there was a window and Scott made his way over to look out at the storm. He felt lucky to be indoors and to have Daphne with him. As he looked out at the storm he wondered what it was that had crashed. The impact was deafening, and left Scott's ears tingling. He didn't notice anyone approaching him until he felt a nudge on his back. Daphne was ready for him, with her bag in hand. "If we leave now we can make it to my dad's place tonight." She called out. Scott heard most of what she was saying and agreed. Daphne's father owned land outside of the city and it would be a good place for them to go to get shelter. He lived alone so it would be good for them to check on him as well. Daphne was a teenager when tragedy struck her family. A car accident claimed the life of her mother and brother, leaving her and her father devastated. They had grown apart despite seeing each other regularly. She had introduced Scott to him and they had gone to dinner a few times since. Daphne knew that she had to go to her father, to make sure he was safe.

Together the two of them drove in the rain, without any radio to listen to. The stations were all off the air as well. They had no connection to the world, but they had each other.

Ben drove with determination through the dark streets. Rain fell faster as the wind picked up. Lightning strikes and headlights of other cars on the road helped light his path. His neighborhood was dark but that didn't stop the residents from prepping for the storm. Some were outside throwing sandbags in front of their garage doors and windows. Other families were loading their vehicles up by flashlight as Ben cruised by. His driveway was now in site and through the darkness he recognized the two cars parked side by side. He braced himself and stepped out into the puddle of rain forming on the ground. Lightning flashed in the sky followed by the rumble of thunder. Ben's hand gripped his keys tight as he approached the front door. He got the door unlocked and stepped inside to the darkness. His dog Kota barked at him from the other room. Ben could hear two voices coming from the dark. Hearing Kelly's voice was comforting to Ben as he approached her. She was with her friend Dana, the daughter of Donald C. Webb, who owned Paragon Car Wash. The two women had candles lit and placed around them in the kitchen. The cabinets were all opened and bags of food were collecting on the table. Ben stood in the archway of their kitchen and knocked on the wall for attention. Both women stopped what they were doing and turned to see the soaked Ben standing there. Kelly's smile was visible in the dim light as she moved towards her man. Ben moved in unison and the two of them shared a hug followed by a kiss. Ben's clothes were soaking Kelly but she held onto him regardless. "I hate to break up the reunion you guys, but we can't forget what we were doing," Dana chimed in. Her hands were full and she had blankets thrown over her shoulder and pillows under her arm. Kelly and Ben let go of each other as she made her way to the bags of supplies on the table. "Does anyone want to fill me in?" Ben questioned. He looked around at the collection of supplies the women had gathered. Besides the food, they had raided the medical cabinet and bathroom items. Suitcases of clothes stacked by the backdoor as Dana threw blankets and pillows on top. "If you had been here with your wife last night you would already know," Dana answered Ben. Kelly looked at her husband who was noticeably upset by the comment. "Ben, it's okay," Kelly reassured him. His face softened as he turned to look at her. Dana scoffed. Ben said in a softer tone, "I'm sorry I couldn't be here last night, I got stuck in the car wash." Kelly approached him and grabbed his hand. Dana scoffed again adding, "Meanwhile your wife was home alone while the sky is falling." Kelly turned to Dana and replied, "You were here with me, and Ben is here now. That's all that matters." Ben felt like saying more but he knew that Dana meant well, and that she was about to back off. He was curious though what she had meant by the sky was falling. After all it was tornado season and they had seen worse storms. "Well what matters is that we make it to the country club before they close the doors" Dana said in a lighter tone. Ben thought about all the times he had gone to play golf with his boss Donald C. Webb at his country club. The clubhouse was a massive building sitting at the top of a hill, with the greens spread out all around it. He had never seen such a beautiful place, and the food was out of this world. "Did your father want us to meet him there?" Ben asked. Dana reached in her purse and pulled out a key card. "Daddy and his friends had the clubhouse renovated to withstand anything. Below it there are three floors of safe rooms that can only be accessed with one of these." She said waving the key card. "Not all of the members have the privilege of this kind of access. Daddy said you're invited to come." Ben was actually surprised by this. He knew that Mr. Webb liked him but if what Dana said was true then this was a good opportunity for them. Ben began to ask, "Why do we need to take shelter like this? My phone hasn't been on so I don't know what the weather is like, but it can't be that bad." Kelly and Dana looked at each other then back at Ben. "Honey," Kelly explained, "let's just say the world is ending."

Chapter Four

THE STREETS WERE BEGINNING TO FLOOD AND THE TRAFFIC HAD picked up as Scott and Daphne made their way out of the city. Their small car was full of things from Scott's apartment, and thanks to Scott, the smell of marijuana. Daphne had objected to him smoking in her car but he did it anyway. The passenger window was open to vent out the smoke as rain fell inside. The windshield wipers were at top speed and still struggled to provide visibility.

Daphne had both hands tentatively on the wheel as she leaned forward to see. Scott finished smoking and resumed what he had been doing. Daphne's father lived eighty five miles from them and if they were lucky, away from the storm. The wind was difficult to deal with as a big truck passed them on the left. Scott asked Daphne if she wanted to continue. She looked over at him in the passenger seat, with a small board game in his lap.

"You have a head and a torso, want to go for an arm?" Scott teased, holding up his pocket edition of Hangman. The magnetic set was perfect for road trips.

Tiago couldn't find any parking in the hospital's garage. He parked his van down the street in the rain. "What do you think?" David asked, showing a drawing he had finished on the drive. He had sketched a wide sword shaped like a feather. "Why a feather?" Al cried out. David shrugged. "Why not make it a wing," Javier suggested. Al nodded, "Yeah that's so cool!" the youngest brother agreed. Tiago opened his door and motioned for his sons to follow. The four of them walked through the rain toward the hospital. The city was dark but they could see the light inside the building. David and Javier were in front leading the way as Al huddled up next to his father. Tiago was eager to get out of the rain and to be with his wife. Hospital procedures allowed for her family to seek shelter during disasters.

They were one block away from the hospital as something fell out of the sky. It was too dark to make out the shape of it but it fell fast and struck the top floors of the hospital. The power went out inside as the force of the impact shook everything nearby. Tiago and his sons were knocked to the ground as the building in front of them went up in smoke and flames. The rain beat down on them as Tiago's heart sank. His wife was inside that building and he had to go to her. Javier and Al helped him to his feet as David ran ahead to the building. Tiago turned to his two boys and demanded they go back to the van. He gave the keys to his oldest son as rain concealed the boy's tears.

Inside the hospital there was a loud explosive noise as the building lit up again and then faded out. The rain prevented Tiago from seeing his son David who had gone ahead. Javier picked up Al and went back to the car as Tiago made his way to his wife.

Ben's car came to a stop outside the tall iron gates of Landry Country Club. There was a small gatehouse outside where a guard would attend the gate, but it was vacant. He turned to Dana who was sitting in the backseat alongside his dog, Kota.

"What now?" Ben asked. Dana had designer sunglasses on despite the dark storms outside. Her hand slipped into her purse and she grabbed the key card from earlier.

"Use this to get inside the gatehouse and open the gate. It works on any door here." She extended the card out to Ben. He ran through the rain and over to the gatehouse. The card was heavier than he imagined it would be. It was solid black with gold engraved on it, Dana's name and the number 21 beside it. He inserted it into the slot on the door and sure enough the door unlocked.

Inside the dark gatehouse there was a desk and office chair. A mini refrigerator sat in the corner with a microwave on top. There was a sliding window on the side where members would pull in to have their IDs checked. Below the window was another card scanner. Ben scanned the card and the gate outside slowly began to open. He ran back through the stormy weather and got in the car. It was a long drive up the hill and to the clubhouse. Trees lined each side of the road as the light from the top of the hill came into view. There was a tall clock tower in the center of a pond, with parking all around the building. Tennis courts were in the back beside the pool area. It was beautiful in the sunlight but on a dark Wednesday like this, it wasn't much to look at.

Dana took back her key card and was the first inside as Kelly and Ben unloaded their car. Kelly held a dog leash in one hand and a bag in the other while Ben carried the rest. Inside the building they made their way into the main dining hall, stopping at the fireplace. Dana brushed her key card against the wall beside the fireplace. The inner wall was made of stone and parted in the middle revealing a secret elevator. All three of them stepped inside as Dana used her card to activate it. Kota sniffed the stone wall before entering. The doors closed in front of them as they descended. When the doors came open a bright light and music greeted them. As they stepped out Ben heard a familiar voice. Approaching them was Dana's father and his boss, Donald C. Webb.

Dana removed her sunglasses and then hugged her father. "Welcome guys, I'm glad we could have you." Mr. Webb said with a smile, his arm around his daughter's shoulder. "Let me show you guys your room." Mr. Webb turned to lead the group.

Still on the road Scott had found himself behind the wheel. Daphne was in the passenger seat cuddling a pillow. He was unsure if she was awake but he tried his best not to disturb her. The road was hard to see as more and more cars had pulled to the side with hazard lights flashing. Scott worried he might hit someone if he was not careful. He found entertainment keeping speed with a fellow car on the highway. They maintained the same speeds together and had gone through several miles together. Scott's mind wandered and he found himself worrying about his family back home. Daphne twitched in the seat beside Scott, startling him. He gripped the steering wheel and focused on the road. There was a streak in the sky as Scott's world lit up. Daphne woke up as Scott swerved, he was looking out the window as something passed overhead. Daphne looked out as a fireball crashed in the distance. "Scott, slow down!" She yelled. The small car was coming to a stop as the car Scott had been traveling with did the same. Daphne jumped out of the passenger side and ran through the rain. She looked out over the guardrail as Scott got out. The other driver was standing in the door frame of his car looking over the roof. Scott came up next to Daphne and put his arm around her. What looked like the wing of a plane burned in the field beside them. Above their heads more debris fell from the sky, but Scott was unable to make out its origin.

Tiago ran through the halls of the first floor. The hospital was dark and there were screams and people running everywhere. He yelled David's name but he could not see his son. He yelled out for his wife but he couldn't hear a response over the noise. Tiago began to look for the stairs so he could find a way to the upper floors where the real damage was. He found the door to the stairwell as someone nudged him from behind. Before he could turn around, his son David's arms were around him. "Sorry I ran off, Pop," David cried out. Tiago hugged the boy, "It's okay," he released his son, "Let's go find your mother." The two of them ran up the stairs and to the second floor. David tried to check with the nurses station but everyone was so busy that the station was deserted. Tiago ran through the halls and someone yelled at him to slow down. There were loud noises coming from the floors above them as screams were getting louder. It sounded like gunfire through the screams. David found his father again who grabbed him and pulled him into a room. "Stay here," He scolded his son. David nodded as his father continued, "I'll find your mother and come back. If I'm not back in five minutes then you go back the way we came in, understand?" Tiago directed his son to nod in agreement. Tiago turned and ran out of the room as David shut the door behind him. A raspy voice broke the silence in the room as

David turned to an elderly lady in the bed behind him. "Well, hello there," She said. There were several machines around her as she struggled to breathe. David was nervous as he approached her. He managed to speak, "Hi, I'm David." She raised her hand and motioned for his. David held hands with her as she spoke, "David, will you do me a favor and find my purse?"

Tiago found himself on the third floor where things seemed to have settled down. The floor was smokey and dark, the windows in the rooms and halls were all blown out. Tiago crouched through the smoke and covered his mouth. He wanted to yell out for his wife but he wasn't sure how safe that was. He wasn't sure what was even going on but he felt the danger looming around him. There was a feeling that Tiago was being watched. His eyes darted around as he did his best to make out everything in the smoke. He heard a noise and moved into a room as flashlights shined down the hallway. Something in his head told him to stay quiet so he did. The lights faded away and a minute passed before Tiago came out from hiding. He was giving up hope as he searched until he heard his name called out. Tiago turned around but he was alone. He yelled out, "Maria-Amor!" There was silence. He looked in every direction. There was one more floor she could be on, and he hoped she wasn't there during the crash. Tiago tried to find his way back to the stairwell when the floor above him exploded. The ceiling came down on him as smoke and fire surrounded him. He was lucky to receive only minor injury as he got out from under the debris. Rain found its way inside through the holes in the ceiling. The sky was visible as the hospital above him was gone. Tiago didn't know what to do anymore.

There was no way his wife survived that. How could he face his sons alone after that? He fell to his knees and lost sight of his surroundings until he was being grabbed by three dark figures. His sons had found each other and made their way to the third floor together. Tiago cried as they all hugged in the darkness.

Ben and Kelly were getting comfortable in their room as Dana and her father left them alone. They were instructed to join them for dinner when they were ready. Their room felt very much like a hotel room. It included a queen sized bed and desk, with a mini fridge and recliner chair. Ben removed his wet clothes as Kelly unpacked their belongings. Kelly laughed and teased Ben that they have showers available. Ben noticed that he had an odor from spending the night in the car wash and decided to shower. Once he finished he dressed and joined his wife to go have dinner with the Webb's. Kota had made himself comfortable on the bed. Donald and his daughter Dana were having dinner in the main hall of the bunker, on the third floor. The room was at capacity with all the tables filled with families. The staff stood by ready to serve them. Ben and Kelly sat down and water was brought to them immediately. Mr. Webb was enjoying a salad as he waited for his dinner to arrive. A server brought over another bowl of salad and plates for the new guests. Ben finally ate for the first time that day. Kelly began to look around the room as she worried about her father. He was, after all, a member at Landry Country Club as well. "Mr. Webb?" She asked as Ben finished his salad. Mr. Webb looked up from his food. "Excuse me," He chuckled, "You guys must have a ton of questions." Kelly nodded and glanced at Ben. A server appeared again with Mr. Webb's dinner, a prime cut steak and potatoes. Dana smiled as her salmon was presented to her. Mr. Webb looked at the young couple and smiled, "Please, order whatever you'd like tonight," He said as he cut his steak. "Where's my father?" Kelly asked anxiously. Mr. Webb picked up his steak with his fork. "What do you mean?" He asked while taking a bite. Kelly looked over at Dana who was busy picking at her dinner. "Well, is my dad a part of this group or what?" She asked looking around, "Because I don't see him." Mr. Webb finished chewing his steak and sipped his wine. "Kelly, it's okay. Your dad, Mike, he didn't want to buy his way into this. So no, he's not here." Mr. Webb said in a serious tone. Dana took a bite out of her food as Ben wondered when his order would be taken. Kelly leaned forward, "Well, then why are *we* here?" she countered. Mr. Webb looked at everyone at the table and back to Kelly. "For two reasons," he began, "One is my daughter asked to bring you, and two is I like Ben. He does good work for me." Ben smiled hearing his boss say that. "As for your dad, don't worry. I bet he's riding out the apocalypse at that big house of his or at the dealership. We both know how much he loves that place," Mr. Webb joked. Ben was more curious than ever, his wife had commented on the world ending but never went into any detail. He figured she was exaggerating the storm. "Mr. Webb," Ben interrupted, "what do you mean by apocalypse?" Ben felt lost as Mr. Webb's face filled with remorse. "Ben, what do you think is happening out there son?" He asked the younger man. Ben looked at his wife, "I don't know, tornado season?" Ben chuckled. He looked back to Mr. Webb who wasn't smiling. "Whatever is happening out there, the weather isn't our worries." Mr. Webb said, wiping his mouth. "Our country is being attacked and all major cities have been destroyed.

Gone." Everyone at the table was quiet. Ben didn't want to believe it. "But I-'' Ben started to speak but he was cut off. "But you what?" Mr. Webb spoke over him. "You didn't hear about it on the news? Or online? That's because there's no one to report on it. Yesterday all our satellites went down." Mr. Webb was getting louder as he talked. "We're down here to survive! Don't you get it? Get comfortable because it's going to be a long stay once we close those doors tonight." Ben couldn't believe what Mr. Webb was telling him. Could it be true? He looked at his wife who confirmed what Mr. Webb was saying. Why was he finding this out so late?

Daphne's car sped on down the highway as they got closer to her father's house. They were halfway there as traffic came to a standstill. The couple had not said much to each other since witnessing the crash together. Scott was in the passenger seat trying to sleep as Daphne tapped on the steering wheel. There was no music so she had to improvise, struggling to keep a good beat. Car horns honked nearby as Daphne became impatient. "We could walk," She said. Scott could tell she was annoyed so he reached into his bag. "What are you doing?" She questioned as he pulled something out. Scott looked up at her, "You need to smoke, it'll help you relax." He replied. He began to pull out a rolling paper. "Of course you'd want to do that right now." She remarked. The car ahead of them moved forward. A few minutes later the cab of the car was full of smoke and Daphne felt better. They found themselves moving again as they passed deep water on the road. It wasn't long until they were getting off the highway. The country roads were dangerous and flooded. Daphne knew the area so she took several detours on the back roads until she found her dad's land. When they pulled up they were surprised to find he wasn't alone, as there were several cars parked outside. Daphne's father had a grill going on the side of the building despite the rain. Scott fell in love with the smell of the meat's cooking. Daphne unloaded her bags as Scott grabbed his. "If you're going to smoke," She warned, "Sneak out here and do it." Scott agreed to her demands. As they approached in the rain the side door swung open and Daphne's father stepped out. He had tongs in one hand and beer in the other. He was surprised to see his daughter and raised his arms in excitement. Daphne wasn't used to this kind of welcome since she lost her family. "Hey, my girls here!" He cried out, "Come get inside and meet everyone!" he yelled. As they approached he put his beer hand around his daughter to hug her. "Hey, Scott," The elder man said as Scott shook his hand and replied, "good to see you, Jim."

Javier and his brothers helped their father into the car. None of them wanted to say a word about their mother. They were all struggling to keep it inside. Tiago was quiet as they strapped him in. Javier turned the keys to the ignition and looked at David in the passenger seat.

"Did you see anything in there?" Javier asked his brother. David looked down at the floorboard and then up to his brother. He shook his head yes. David thought about the old lady in the hospital room. She knew she was dying and she didn't have much time left. She instructed David to get her purse and once she had it she dug inside pulling out a small card. She put it in David's hand and told him where to go. She promised he would be safe there and that he could bring his family as well.

Javier asked his brother what he saw. David didn't say anything but he pulled out a black card from his pocket. "An old woman said to use this before midnight," He finally spoke. Javier grabbed the card and looked back at the burning hospital behind them. He knew that with the loss of their mother Tiago would need his help more than ever. He had to be strong for his brothers, no matter how much Javier wanted to cry.

"Okay, you know where we're going?" Javier asked as he put the car in drive. David started to tear up as Al cried in the backseat. "She told me everything we need to do to survive." David said as they drove off from the hospital.

Chapter Five

SCOTT AND DAPHNE WERE RELIEVED THAT THE ELECTRICITY WAS on in her father's home. They showered together and changed into dry clothes to join her father for dinner. Jim was surrounded by his friends and Daphne felt comfort that he had them around. Scott shook hands with her father once more before making himself a plate of food. Daphne hugged her father and he kissed her forehead. There was something different about him Daphne couldn't figure out. "Come on, I'll introduce you to everyone," Jim spoke in a lighter tone. Daphne followed her father into the other room as Scott finished preparing his plate. "Jim, who is this?" A man asked as Daphne and her father approached. There were a few men sharing a couch with beers in hand. Two other men sat at a table in the back, leaned over a game of chess. "Fellas, this is my daughter I've told ya about," Jim began, "This is Daphne." Everyone stood up while Jim introduced them, "This is Craig, Bob, Dave, and Tom." Daphne said hello to each of them as they shook hands. She already knew the fifth man in the room, Mr. Bolton. She remembered growing up with Mr. Bolton's son, Nathan. Daphne gave Mr. Bolton a hug as Scott entered the room. He introduced himself as well and everyone sat down again. Cold beers were dispersed around the room. Scott chowed down on his dinner while Daphne opened a beer.

"I'm telling you, if they wanted to, they could control the weather," Dave spat out his words. He was looking for his chance to continue an earlier argument. Craig shook his head in dispute as Tom voiced his doubt, "Dave, we get it. You love your conspiracy theories." Tom had returned to his chess game with Mr. Bolton and moved his knight as he spoke. Mr. Bolton laughed quietly as he looked at the game board. Daphne was picking a piece of chicken from Scott's plate as the men continued. Dave carried on, "Okay Tom, well what do you have to say about what's happening right now in America?" Tom looked over at Dave on the couch and shouted, "This is different and you know it!"

Daphne and Scott looked at each other confused. *This is escalating quickly,* Scott thought.

Mr. Bolton knocked on the table to get Tom's attention back on their game. Daphne wanted to know more about what these men were talking about. She asked, "What's going on exactly?" Jim turned and looked at his daughter. "Honey," he said, surprised, "Don't you guys Know?" Daphne shook her head. "Wow. Okay," Jim sighed. "Well first of all," Jim began but Dave interrupted saying, "This storm is a cover up to divert us away from the city." Jim glared at the conspiracy theorist and finished telling Daphne what was happening. "Yesterday all our satellites were wiped out. Before communications were disabled we heard every major city was gone. They were just gone in an instant. They don't know what kind of attack it was but this is the worst in American history." Daphne had tears in her eyes as the news sunk in. Mr. Bolton spoke up, "It's true. My son barely made it home this morning." Scott stopped eating as he thought about his family. The two of them hugged each other as some of the men sipped their beer in silence. Dave broke the silence with more of his theories, "I'm not speaking ill of the dead now. What country on Earth has that kind of firepower?" Craig spoke up, "Dave, I'm getting tired of listening to you." Jim stood up and tried to ease the tension, "I know what everybody needs," He said leaving the room. A moment later Jim returned with a small wooden box. Scott had continued eating but he still worried about his family. There was no way he could contact them. He just had to have hope. Jim sat back down and opened his box to reveal a pipe and a bag of marijuana. Daphne was shocked to see her father doing such a thing. She thought for a second it may have been Scott's and her dad found it, but the pipe was foreign to her. Scott smiled and enjoyed the look on Daphne's face. "Dad," She exclaimed, "When did you start smoking?" He smiled and loaded his pipe, "I could ask you the same thing," he quipped. As they passed the pipe around the storm outside continued. Dave obviously had more to say and Scott was interested to hear some of it. When Dave got up to go to the kitchen Scott followed him. Dave started to make a plate of food as Scott approached him. "You mind if I ask what you think is happening out there?" Scott asked. Dave looked up from the plate he was preparing and their eyes met. "I think it's something out of this world, here to invade us," Dave said seriously. The back door swung open startling the men as someone stepped inside. "I'm sorry, but I heard what you said," the newcomer confessed before adding, "You think it's aliens?" Dave stood firm and nodded defending his statement. "You're crazy, old man," replied the newcomer. The young man moved through the kitchen leaving Scott and Dave. Scott wondered who this guy was as Daphne called out in the other room, "Nathan! Oh my god!" Scott left Dave alone in the kitchen to join the others. Daphne was hugging her old friend as Scott reunited with her. "Scott, this is Mr. Bolton's son. We grew up together." Daphne declared as the two men shook hands. "Nice to meet you, Scott," Nathan said as their handshake ended. "You too," Scott replied. Nathan was taller than Scott and had an athletic figure. His hair was short and kept neat. He turned to his father, Mr. Bolton, who was still playing chess. "Come on. I gotta take you home. Mom's orders," Nathan said as he put his hand on his father's shoulder. Mr. Bolton looked up from his chess game and at his son. "Nate, why don't you tell these guys what you saw out there," Mr. Bolton said as he motioned for the pipe. Daphne had her arm around Scott's waist as he passed the glass pipe. Nathan grabbed the pipe from his father before he could inhale. "Don't ask me to relive that," Nathan sighed as he put the pipe down on the table. Mr. Bolton stood up and put his hand on his son's shoulder.

Ben and company finished their dinner together at Landry Country Club. Afterwards they were sent back to their room for the evening. Everything happened so fast that Ben felt like it was all a dream. Kelly was silent throughout dinner, and remained that way until bed. The lights in their room cut off after dinner to conserve power so there wasn't much left to do but sleep. Kelly showered in the dark before joining Ben and Kota in bed. Ben laid there with his wife in the dark for half an hour before they rolled over to face each other. Kelly broke the silence and asked if Ben felt like leaving. Ben knew that she was worried about her father but he had his doubts. He leaned in for a kiss and asked her if she would like to take a walk with him. The two of them got up and left their room with Kota. The halls were darker than earlier with limited lights on. The other members had retired to their rooms as well. Ben and Kelly were on the first floor, which was mostly used for lodging. The second floor also had rooms for residents, as well as a small library and game room for the kids. The third floor was the dinner hall and included laundry services and employee quarters. They walked about all three floors together holding hands. As they made their way back to their room they heard shouting coming from the main hall where the elevator was. Curious, they decided to investigate together. A group of members had formed around the elevator and one man was screaming accusations about his mother. Ben and Kelly joined the crowd and heard someone else shouting back at the disgruntled resident. Mr. Webb joined up with them and asked Ben what was going on. Kelly stayed back with Kota while Ben advanced through the crowd with Mr. Webb. In the center a man was accusing a family of stealing his mother's access card. Ben and Mr. Webb pushed closer to see Javier and his family soaked from the rain. David was cursing at the man for leaving his mother in the hospital to die. Ben and Mr. Webb looked at each other before the older man stepped forward. "Everyone, it's okay," He urged in an attempt to calm the group. "Go back to your rooms, this young man and his family are guests of mine," Mr. Webb shouted. The crowd started to disperse as Mr. Webb looked at the man who accused Javier's family. "Young man, what's the problem?" Mr. Webb asked with concern. The younger man looked angry hearing the question. "Mr. Webb, they stole Mother's card, it has her name and number!" He shouted. Mr. Webb grabbed the card from David and examined it. The furious son continued to cry out, "I got the notification that Mother had arrived and I came to greet her. Instead I found these thieves." He handed it back to David. "Well, it looks like they have inherited your mother's room. Would you be kind enough to escort them there?" Mr. Webb instructed. The young man threw his arms in the air and stormed off. He cursed back at Mr. Webb as he left. Javier thanked his boss as Mr. Webb asked for David's card again. He called out and a server came to Mr. Webb who motioned him toward Javier and his family. "You'll be taken to your room now," Mr. Webb reassured the family. Ben and Kelly approached and offered to take them to their room. Mr. Webb stayed behind and spoke to the servant as everyone left.

It was getting late, and as the two Bolton men said their goodbyes, some of the others began to call it a night. Daphne finally got to be alone with the two men that mattered most to her. Jim and Scott had been bonding over marijuana and Scott showed off his collection he had packed. Daphne couldn't believe how fast he had packed earlier and yet he managed to bring all his smoking gear. He had papers to roll with, pipes to smoke with, and even seeds he had collected. She finally became too tired to stay up with them any longer and retreated upstairs to the spare bedroom. Scott joined her not long after.

Ben and Kelly told Javier what they learned that night at dinner as Javier thought about his mother. David and Al remained quiet as they listened to the adults leading them to their new room. The couple left the Rodrigues family alone as they said goodnight. Javier made his brothers take turns showering while he helped his father to relax. He sat Tiago down in a recliner and tried to ask if he needed anything. His father did not reply and instead closed his eyes. Javier felt helpless as he waited for his brothers to get dressed and settled in bed. The teenager stood alone in the shower and cried over the loss of his mother. The water was cold before he finally had the strength to get out and dry off. When he got to bed his brothers were still awake and they all held each other as they drifted off to sleep.

Javier slept like a baby through the night. A nice contrast to the previous night spent in Paragon Car Wash with Scott's snoring. A knock on the door had woke him and his brothers from their sleep. It was Mr. Webb personally inviting them to breakfast. The Rodrigues boys brushed their teeth and headed out to eat. Tiago refused to get out of his chair where he had slept. The breakfast hall was full of people and reminded Javier of being back in the school cafeteria. There were lines of people preparing plates while others sat at tables waiting to be served. Ben and Kelly were already seated at Mr. Webb's table. Dana was there as well and she introduced herself to the boys. David was eyeing the line for food with Al while Mr. Webb waved his server over. It was the same server from the night before. "No need for lines when you're with me," Mr. Webb smiled. A minute later Javier and his brothers had food in front of them. Javier thanked Mr. Webb as his boss went on to pull another key card from his pocket. "I want to apologize for what happened last night," Mr. Webb said, extending his hand for Javier to take the card. Javier did so and Mr. Webb resumed his apology, "As luck would have it, another room opened up. It would be perfect for you and your family, it's the room next to yours." Javier looked down at the heavy card in his hand.

Another room? Javier thought, *Why is he being so generous?*

Mr. Webb sipped on his orange juice and then Dana changed the subject. She talked about the plans they had for community activities later on in the day. The boys were still quiet from their experience the day before. Mr. Webb left with Ben as the two women stayed at the table to finish their cocktails. Javier and his two brothers went back to their room as they compared key cards. Javier's card had the same name registered on it, confirming his suspicion it belonged to the man from the night before. Al laughed and teased, "I hope they kicked that jerk out in the rain!"

Chapter Six

THE RAIN WAS WORKING ON ITS THIRD DAY OF RAMPAGE AS SCOTT and Daphne spent their time cleaning her father's home. The two story house had collected a lot of dust over the years. Daphne had to cover her face to prevent her allergies from attacking. Scott swept the floors and tried his best not to think about Paragon Car Wash. He was relieved to be away from work, although he wished for better circumstances. Guilt flooded his mind as he thought about how horrible it was to be happy about something like that. Jim's house still had power although it would flicker periodically throughout the day. The outside world was a mystery to them, with no way of making contact to know if they were even safe. Jim was downstairs with Daphne when they heard the echo of gunfire coming from the distance. It was faint, and could have been mistaken for something else if it wasn't repeated several more times. Jim yelled from downstairs and charged up to his room, passing Scott. Downstairs Daphne was yelling up to him. Running down the stairs before he knew it, Scott had Daphne in his arms as Jim emerged at the top of the stairs. "Scott, get up here and grab a piece," Jim called down. Scott was nervous as he had never fired a gun before and rarely held one. "is he serious?" Scott mumbled to Daphne as her father slipped back into his room.

Upstairs Scott and Daphne found themselves with a selection of weapons to choose. "It's our right to own guns and protect our land," Jim said with a smile as he dug through his gun safe. It was several feet tall and bigger than his dresser. Scott couldn't argue with Jim about his rights, although this collection seemed excessive to him. Reaching down, Scott grabbed a handgun at random. The pistol was cold and heavier than Scott anticipated. "9mm, good choice," Jim smirked. "Let me get you a holster, you never know when the enemy could be on our doorstep." The old man turned to dig in his safe again.

The enemy? Scott thought. It sunk in that they really were under attack and their country was being invaded.

The electricity flickered again as the three of them armed themselves. Jim put his arsenal away safely as the couple moved downstairs. Daphne knelt down in front of the fireplace and prepared to make a fire. Scott, still unsure about carrying a gun in the house, asked for candles. They couldn't rely on the electricity lasting much longer. Daphne had a fire started and together they arranged candles around the first floor. Jim joined them in front of the fire and sat down on the couch, his wooden box in hand. Scott felt his nerves relaxing as they began to smoke together. Daphne joined them on the couch as the lights went out for the final time.

Jim got up to poke the fire as they heard a vehicle approaching outside. The horn honked several times as the headlights flashed at the windows. "Scott, get your gun out," Jim instructed, drawing his own handgun and moving toward the door. Daphne watched her father peek out the side window and mumble, "false alarm, it's Dave's truck." Jim lowered his weapon and grabbed his jacket from the hook on the wall. Scott looked back at Daphne who was now up from the couch. Jim stepped outside into the rain as Daphne urged Scott to follow him. Wearing one of Jim's extra jackets, Scott stepped out onto the front porch. The sky was dark but the horizon had a fiery glow. Jim was approaching Dave's truck as Scott stayed under the patio for shelter from the rain. In the darkness Scott could see the smoldering passenger side of the pickup truck. Jim shouted at the driver side window and Scott ran out to his aid. The door was open when Scott got there and looked inside. Jim struggled to find his words as Dave turned to look at them in the rain. Dave's right side of his body had fresh burns and the interior of the truck's cab was still smoking. His seat belt melted to his chest and caused him intense pain as he tried to sit forward. Jim had tears swelling in his eyes for his friend. "Bob's dead," Dave cried out through the pain. Scott wanted to cry seeing Dave in pain like this. "Should we get him inside the house?" Scott suggested. Jim thought about it for a second before Dave protested, "Leave me here and save yourselves." Dave groaned as he leaned his head back against the seat. Jim sent Scott inside the house for a knife to cut Dave free from the seat belt. Scott ran inside and Daphne helped him search for a knife. When they found one she offered her help outside but Scott wanted her to be ready when they came back. Outside Jim was walking back to the house. Dave's door now shut and the headlights off. Jim shook his head in disbelief when he saw Scott. "He's gone," Jim confessed. Scott didn't know what to say so he followed Jim in silence back to the house. Daphne helped her father out of his wet jacket as Scott locked the door behind him. Daphne cried as she learned two of her father's friends were dead. Scott began to feel dizzy so he sat down.

Who could be doing this? He kept asking himself.

He looked up from the couch he was sitting on as Daphne and Jim were running from the room. Scott tried to calm himself down as Daphne returned with a tool box. Jim came in with a roll of chicken wire under his arm. Jim and Daphne moved to the windows while Jim shouted at Scott. Jim's voice was angry as he shouted again, "Scott!" Daphne held a staple gun up to the wall while Jim positioned the chicken wire. They were barricading the windows as Scott stood up to join them. "Sorry," Scott apologized, "what can I do?" Jim pulled the wire tight as Daphne finished securing it. Daphne moved to the next window as her father instructed Scott to head back outside. There was extra lumber in the shed from when Jim worked on his fence. Scott threw on his wet jacket from earlier and ran out the side door. Jim made sure to send him out with the key but in the dark Scott struggled to get it open. He could hear a vehicle approaching the house from the front. Scott considered hiding in the shed but decided not to abandon Daphne like that. There was enough fencing to cover the windows but Scott could only carry so much. He made it back to the house and tried to peek in the kitchen window before he entered. His hands were shaking as he shut the door behind him. Unsure of who was outside their home, Scott's priority was getting back to Daphne. He left the wood in the kitchen and moved through the dark house with his hand on his gun. The light from the fireplace shined on the front door which stood ajar. Scott emerged from the darkness of the hall as Jim and Daphne were greeting Nathan Bolton.

It was easy to see by firelight that Nathan was in a panicked state. He was trembling and carried a revolver on his hip. Sweat could have been mistaken for rain beading up on his forehead. Nathan turned to Scott and pleaded, "Tell them it's not safe to stay put like this!" Scott was next to Daphne now and put his arm around her shoulder. "What do you propose we do then?" Jim protested to the young man. Nathan turned back to face Jim and replied, "My parents have been preparing for this for nearly a decade." Outside there was an explosion in the distance. Daphne held onto Scott as Nathan continued, "We have an underground bunker I can take you to, but we have to leave now!" Daphne nodded her head and Scott was willing to do what was necessary for them to be safe. Jim however, felt compelled to stay in his home. He voiced his doubts and protested, "I have my guns here, I'll take my chances," his hand resting on his pistol. Nathan placed his hand on Jim's shoulder and begged, "please Mr. Williams, for your daughter." Daphne took her queue and spoke up, "Dad, please let's just go to the Bolton's." Jim scoffed and sat on the couch. Scott sat next to him and tried to ease the mood, stating, "we can bring our weed." Jim gave him a cold stare. "That reminds me," Jim said as he got up to fetch his pipe. Nathan sighed and knew he had to let them in on what he had been through. Jim returned with his wooden box and sat beside Scott on the couch. Scott had pulled a small container from his own pocket and contributed. Nathan waited until they lit up before confessing to them. "Daphne," he began. "You remember how I was working to get my CDL license?" Nathan asked. Daphne nodded as Jim and Scott passed the pipe. "Well I got it, class A. I've been doing that for awhile now to save up to build my own house on my family's land." Nathan paused for a second before he could continue. "I was making a delivery Tuesday morning, a distribution center outside Oklahoma City," he stated. Jim coughed as smoke escaped his lungs. Nathan tried to proceed but Jim interrupted, asking, "Where's this story going?" Nathan looked insulted but collected himself. "The story is I was on my way into the city and the next thing I knew there wasn't a city in front of me," Nathan revealed. Scott's eyes were on Daphne as she stood by the fire, her face in her palms. As Scott got up to comfort Daphne Nathan continued, his voice was softer. "I saw it," Nathan said. Everyone's eyes were on him as he continued, "All that stuff Dave spouted last night about the attacks. I saw it, before the storms hit." Another explosion could be heard in the distance, further than the last. Scott spoke up, "What are you talking about?" He thought about the alien comment Nathan disregarded the night before. "What did you see?" Daphne asked. "I saw a ship," Nathan declared, "I saw a ship crawl through the sky like nothing I've ever seen before." Scott felt a chill go up his spine. Jim scoffed. "You sound like Dave," Jim said as he knocked the ash from his pipe. Jim's comment angered Nathan as he snapped back, "Yeah, well Dave's dead!" Nathan hesitated before he said his next words. "If I had told y'all yesterday even, maybe the two of them wouldn't be dead," Nathan yelled. Daphne and Scott held each other by the fire. Jim's pipe was reloaded as he remained silent. The flick of his lighter accompanied the crackle of the fireplace. After the ember went out in his pipe Jim stood up. Daphne went to him and put her arms around him for a hug. She looked up at her father and said, "Dad, we should go to Bolton's." Jim shook his head, "No sweetheart, I'm staying here. You and Scott go if you'd like." Daphne pressed him, "but why?" she asked. Jim looked away from his daughter. "Because," he answered, "because this house has all my memories of your brother. And your mother." Jim turned back to face his daughter with teary eyes. "And because I'm dying no matter where I go. I have cancer. That's the reason I started smoking," he confessed. Daphne began to cry as she hugged her father. Scott joined their hug as Nathan checked the windows. "I hate to say it, but if anyone is coming with me then we need to pack up and go, now!" Nathan shouted from the window. Scott and Nathan went upstairs while Daphne stayed with her father. Nathan found a duffel bag inside Jim's gun safe and filled it with everything he could fit inside. Scott joined up with him carrying both his and Daphne's bags. Nathan filled the remaining boxes of ammo from the safe into their bags. The two men headed downstairs to regroup as Daphne had managed to get her father on his feet. They knew Jim could not be convinced to leave his home so the three of them hurried to barricade his windows. "I'll be okay," Jim said as he hugged his daughter. Daphne cried as her father continued, "I want this. You go on and take shelter with Scott and survive whatever this is." Scott hugged Jim as they said goodbye and Nathan returned the safe keys to Jim. "We didn't take it all," Nathan promised, "But my dad will be grateful for what you did." Jim took the keys from Nathan and laughed, "I doubt it, your old man never approved of my gun collection." They shook hands and Daphne ran over to hug her father one last time. "I love you," Jim said through tears. Daphne wiped his tears away, ignoring her own, replying, "I love you, too."

The roads were dark and flooded as Nathan's truck led Scott through the rain. Daphne insisted on taking her car to the Bolton ranch. Scott struggled to see anything in the dark as Daphne stared out the window at the rain. He wanted to say something to comfort her, but he knew it wasn't the time. Scott wanted nothing more than to make her feel like everything was going to be okay. But he knew it wasn't, not anymore. Nathan's truck stopped abruptly in front of them and Scott slammed his foot into the brake pad. The turn signal flashed on Nathan's truck, instructing them to pull off the main road and onto private property. There was a two story house standing next to a large barn as Nathan parked in the front drive. Scott parked behind him and jumped out to unload Daphne's car. Inside the house they made their way into the basement. There was a thick steel door in the dark, and Nathan unlocked it to reveal a ladder going down. Daphne climbed down first while Scott followed close behind. Nathan was the last to go down and he locked the door before his descent. The bunker was bright and smelled like herbs and spices cooking. Daphne and Scott were welcomed by the Bolton family and shown to their sleeping quarters. The family was not alone, as Craig Callahan from the night before was there with his two young kids. Craig tried to ask about Jim but Daphne ignored him. Scott explained what they had gone through and Craig left them alone to get some rest. Daphne and Scott had a small cot to share but they cuddled close as she cried herself to sleep. Scott drifted off not long after.

Gunshots in the distance pulled them out of their sleep. Scott had no clue what was happening or how much time had passed. Daphne wasted no time getting into her backpack that she stashed below the cot. She pulled out Scott's 9mm handgun and passed it to him as she removed hers as well. Craig and his children were one room over, hiding in their sleeping quarters. Scott held Daphne's hand and ran towards the exit.

They found Mrs. Bolton in the kitchen, still cooking dinner. Nathan and his father were shouting in the next room. Scott joined up with them as Daphne stayed with Mrs. Bolton. "Scott," Nathan sounded relieved as he spoke, "Come check out that gunfire with me." Scott thought Nathan was crazy and looked to Mr. Bolton for his opinion. "I don't want you going out there, Nate," Mr. Bolton argued. Nathan wasn't listening as he motioned Scott to follow him. Scott watched as Nathan climbed the ladder up to the basement and felt like hiding with Craig. Instead he took a deep breath and followed Nathan into danger. The basement was dark and with all the time Scott had spent in the dark lately he figured it wouldn't be as spooky. The unknown danger of chasing gunfire made the hairs on Scott's neck stand up. He had his pistol in his hand but he hoped to God he wouldn't have to use it. Not that he knew how. Nathan seemed more calm and collected as he crouched through the dark. He led the way for Scott as they climbed the staircase into the house.

Where is he leading me? Scott thought. He had not been this nervous in a long time.

They were in the Bolton house, standing in the kitchen as rain beat into the windows outside. Scott hoped they would not find anything as more gunfire erupted directly outside. Nathan ran to the window and crouched below it. He peaked out as he raised his own gun. One last gunshot rang out as Scott jumped under the table. Nathan began to crawl towards the backdoor as he heard something approach the house. He had his gun ready as there was a knock at the backdoor. Nathan looked over to Scott for backup but it was clear he had none. His gun raised and his trigger finger ready, Nathan slowly stood up. His back was pressed against the refrigerator for cover as the Knock grew louder. A voice screamed outside but it was muffled and unfamiliar. Nathan moved closer as the voice became clearer. Tom, his dad's friend, stood at the backdoor shouting nonsense as Nathan let him in. The man was dripping from the rain and had blood on his shirt as well as what appeared to be tar. Tom's hands would not let go of his double barrel shotgun as Nathan tried to calm him down. Scott realized they were not being attacked and made his way out from under the table. Together the two of them helped Tom get down into the basement and finally down to the bunker. Daphne kissed Scott when he returned and Mrs. Bolton prepared coffee for everyone. Tom was mumbling to himself as Craig came to check on the commotion. Dinner was put on hold in the bunker as everyone sipped coffee and tried to make sense of what Tom was mumbling. Half an hour passed before Tom became coherent. Mr. Bolton sat down in a chair across the table from his friend and asked whose blood was on his shirt. Tom stared at him while tears swelled up in his eyes. Tom's voice cracked as he said, "My family." Mrs. Bolton gasped from the kitchen. Tom's face was pale as he spoke, "My family, they took my family." He stood up, "I killed one of 'em. They took my wife and daughter and then chased me here." Scott looked over at Nathan who looked ready for a fight. Mr. Bolton tried to say something as Tom ran to the exit. Mr. Bolton stood as he called out, "who took your family?"

Tom glanced back, "Aliens took my family," he confessed, "And I killed one of those sons o' bitches on your doorstep." Scott and Nathan followed close behind as Tom led them outside. All of Scott's fear earlier had transitioned into curiosity. The three men traveled outside into the rain together. It was dark but the body was visible.

This is really happening, Scott thought.

There was no question Tom had killed someone out there in the dark and the rain. Nathan kicked the body as Scott gripped his gun. He felt like they were being watched as Tom helped Nathan pick up the corpse. They carried it inside the house and out of the rain. Scott's curiosity was escalating as they laid it on the kitchen table. Nathan pulled a flashlight from his back pocket and flashed it on the head of the grey body. Scott threw up in his mouth. It was shorter than he'd expected, not even five feet if he had to guess. It's head was round like a human, but it lacked a nose and ears. There was a wound on the right side of the skull, where a bullet had grazed it. The chest was narrow, with two more bullet wounds oozing with the same tar from Tom's shirt. Scott touched the corpse's suit, a dark material surrounded the entire body. Nathan cursed to himself. Scott's hand touched the deceased face as he traced his fingertip from its strong jawline up to its brow. The body was warm and hairless. Scott felt inclined to place his palm on the forehead just above its large eyes. The contact caused Scott harm, as his head began to pound. Scott's vision blurred as the dead alien's eyelids opened. Scott blacked out and collapsed to the floor as the alien on the table sat up.

Chapter Seven

JAVIER AND HIS BROTHERS MADE THEMSELVES AT HOME WITHIN THE walls of Landry. The bunker provided nearly three hundred residents with shelter according to Mr. Webb. The staff was close to one hundred of the Country Club's most loyal employees. They had the privilege of bringing their families with them into the massive bunker. Javier put their second room to good use as he separated his two brothers. They had not said much since they arrived, none of them had. Tiago remained in his chair, tuning out the world around him. Javier left David with their father and moved into the neighboring suite with Al. The two rooms were identical right down to the last detail. Javier had filled up on breakfast so he stayed behind in his room as Al went to the community room to meet the other kids. Javier broke down in tears. He felt the weight of his responsibilities crushing down on his shoulders. His family mattered most to him in this world, and losing his mother was proving to be difficult for his father. Javier sat up on the bed and wiped his eyes, they were beat red as he made contact with his reflection in the mirror. He chuckled to himself and thought about Scott. He would no doubt be making a comment about Javier's red eyes, and where he could get some of what he had been smoking. Javier realized that he may never see Scott again, if the world outside was as bleak as the description. The rest of

Javier's day went by and it was uneventful. He listened to Al talk about the kids he met inside the bunker and had dinner with his brothers. Mr. Webb was nowhere to be seen at lunch or at dinner, neither was Ben. Javier did see Kelly Miller, and she was as beautiful as he remembered. He spent his dinner watching her from across the room as she conversed with Mr. Webb's daughter. Afterwards he checked on his father before lights out.

Ben Miller had been in the bunker for two days before Mr. Webb put him to work. To Ben's surprise most of the funding for the bunker underneath Landry had been provided by Mr. Webb. The Landry family themselves had a small investment according to Mr. Webb. Ben found himself managing the entire staff, which made him feel proud after all his hard work at Paragon. Mr. Webb was finally giving him the credit he deserved. Ben understood why he had to work, food And shelter for him and his wife wasn't going to come free after all. Still, Ben felt guilty spending most of his time away from Kelly. She had Dana Webb to keep her company but they had little time for each other while the lights were on. As Kelly fell asleep in Ben's arms that night his mind wandered. He thought about his bank account of all things, his paycheck was due to direct deposit soon. It would be Friday morning when he woke up and Ben could not believe the world outside was gone. He held his wife tight as he drifted off to sleep.

Friday morning came and Javier found himself greeted at the door by Ben Miller. Al was excused to go to breakfast but Ben asked that Javier report to work. This came as a surprise to Javier as he was hungry and not prepared to work first thing in the morning. Ben explained that

Mr. Webb wanted everyone to pull their weight around the bunker. Javier and his family had been lucky enough to get in the way that they did. Javier reluctantly agreed for the sake of his family. Ben informed Javier that he would be working in the kitchen during the morning. As Javier began to leave Ben approached the other Rodrigues suite. Javier was within earshot as he heard Ben ask for David to report to work. Turning around swiftly Javier protested, "He's Fourteen. You can't make him work!" David looked on as Javier came to his defense. Ben sighed, "He's old enough to contribute. Mr. Webb said thirteen and up." Tiago, who had been in his chair the entire stay at Landry, began to twitch about. He heard the commotion outside his door and went to his son's aid. Tiago looked Ben in the eyes and declared, "you will not make my son work. David, get inside." the fourteen year old did as his father demanded. Ben shook his head and matched Tiago's gaze. "You have a position here as well, Mr. Rodrigues," Ben remarked. Javier's eyes were on his father. Tiago scoffed and replied, "No thanks." Ben could tell Tiago would not have it any other way. He relaxed a little and assured Tiago that he would be back tomorrow.

Mr. Webb was having lunch by the time Ben met up with him. Eating lunch with Kelly would have been nice but Ben continued his work. "I have Javier working the kitchen sir, but his family was difficult," Ben confessed. Mr. Webb smiled as he cut into his steak. The food smelled amazing. Ben had a steak dinner the first night but since then the food had declined. "I need you working tonight," Mr. Webb said as he chewed, "after lights out. We have some members Staying with us that are overstaying their welcome." Ben immediately thought about Javier's family. "Are you paying attention?" Mr. Webb asked before continuing, "some of our guests scoffed at the idea of building this bunker. Well, you get what you pay for. Check out will be tonight." A soft napkin in Mr. Webb's hand wiped at the corners of his mouth while he spoke. "Round them up. Starting tomorrow we go for the staff and their families. I want you to make me a list of your best workers. They can stay for now, the food down here won't last forever. We have to make hard decisions and look after our own now." Mr. Webb sounded content, not the least bit remorseful. Ben swallowed the lump in his throat that had formed. Ben was dismissed to eat his own lunch before continuing his day.

Javier's time in the kitchen went by rather fast. He found comfort in the mundane work. Most of the kitchen staff left him alone once he got started, and once his shift ended he didn't waste time leaving. Back in his room he found his father and his brothers preparing their things. Tiago was rushing his son's to get ready. Javier approached his father and asked him to stop what he was doing. Tiago dismissed his oldest son and told him they were leaving tonight after lights out.

Ben's room smelled sweet like Kelly's perfume when he finally returned home. Kota greeted his person at the door with a wet tongue and wagging tail. Kelly was gone, most likely with Dana Webb. Ben took Kota for a walk in the halls and made his way to the small indoor park built on the second floor. The park had a playground for the kids with two trees and a dedicated area for pets. Kota was a happy dog as he walked with Ben back to their room. Ben used his free time to nap in bed before Kelly returned home. When Ben woke up he was happy to find Kelly resting beside him. She was awake, and her eyes sparkled as her smile spread across her face. Ben leaned forward and kissed his wife on the lips. He was unsure how long he had slept until Kelly told him to join her for dinner. She sat up in bed and braided her red hair. Ben got up and used the bathroom while his wife got ready. Tonight after dinner he would have to meet up with Mr. Webb and then force people out of the bunker. Families would be kicked out in the rain and the unknown. Ben thought of Javier and his family, Mr. Webb would kick them out for sure if they did not work soon.

Over the course of dinner Javier and his brothers convinced their father to stay in Landry. Al was a crier and without the support of his wife it was more than enough to sway Tiago. It was decided that they would give it the weekend before making any decisions.

Lights out came and the Rodrigues family called it a night as well. At the same time Ben was saying goodnight to Kelly and Kota. When Kelly confronted her husband about his plans for the night Ben chose to lie. His wife's kiss provided more comfort than she realized as they said goodbye. Ben walked down the hall to a neighboring room. His knock was steady as he summoned the inhabitants. The door swung open and two men emerged from the darkness. "Mr. Webb sent me," Ben informed the men. The two men nodded and one of them stepped back inside Their dark room. Ben recognized that man from his first night in Landry. He was personally serving Mr. Webb that day. The man who remained with Ben was a strong build with a dark beard, through which he spoke, "We know. I'm Matt and this is my brother, call him T. '' Ben's eyes left Matt's as his attention fell on T returning from their room. In T's hand was a small pistol, which he began to holster on his waist. Ben feared what would happen should they need to use that thing. The three of them proceeded down the hallway to fulfill Mr. Webb's orders.

Over an hour passed as they went door to door and notified families that they were no longer welcome. The news came as a surprise with the exception being a few curse words directed towards Mr. Webb. The tenants cooperated with the gun wielding men who brought them to the main entrance. Ben used Mr. Webb's key card to open the metal elevator doors. One by one he sent families out into the dangers of the surface world. The last family got into the elevator, the children were crying. The father held onto his daughter as he stared Ben in the eyes. running his fingers through his daughter's hair the father spoke, "what will you do when they come for you? When it's your family on this elevator?" Ben didn't have an answer as the metal doors slid shut. Ben and the two brothers were finished for the night. They returned to their rooms Without saying a word to one another. Kota greeted Ben at the door but he gave his dog no attention. He showered in the dark but his actions that night left him feeling dirty. Kelly was in bed asleep as Ben joined her. He considered the words of the father he exiled, and what he would be willing to do for Kelly. It was dark but he could see her peaceful face beside him. Ben knew he would be willing to kill if it meant keeping her safe.

Chapter Eight

SCOTT CARTER DROPPED TO THE COLD TILE IN THE BOLTON
kitchen. Leaping down from the table was the odd lanky body of an
alien warrior. Nathan and Tom looked in confusion as the alien let out a
chilling whistle. The sound soon became unnerving as it echoed the cry
of a child's scream. Nathan pulled his gun on the grey skinned alien
standing before him. The alien lacked in stature but it's haunting whistle
continued as its arms raised up lunging at Nathan. Before he could ready
himself the alien had swatted Nathan's gun away and it slid across the
floor. Alien arms came down swiftly on the Bolton son as Tom stood
frozen watching the attack unfold. Tom was sure he had shot this
creature dead. Nathan blocked the swings of the square jawed alien and
did what came natural. He planted his feet as his boots squeaked on the
floor. Nathan Bolton's hands flew through the air, each time connecting
blows with the alien. The grey creature was overwhelmed by Nathan's
size and power. It tried to swing back but out of nowhere Tom tackled
the alien to the floor. "I had him!" Nathan cried out as he flexed his sore
knuckles. Tom held down the alien while replying back, "this thing can
tell me where they took my family!" Tom's brow was sweaty. The
pinned alien had been silent since Nathan's barrage of fists began. "You
heard that thing, there won't be much talking," Nathan retorted. Out of

the darkness Daphne Williams appeared. She recognized her man on the floor and went to his aid. "What the hell is going on up here?" Daphne questioned from the floor. Her hand ran through Scott's hair, brushing it off of his forehead. Nathan had his flashlight and turned it to reveal the alien pinned below Tom. "This guy attacked us," Nathan said, explaining the alien on the floor. Daphne wanted to scream but she kept it together. "This is the alien I told y'all about. The one I killed," Tom jested. Daphne glanced down to the alien and then back to Tom. "Good job," she quipped. Nathan took a more serious tone, "let's take this thing down to the basement. We got some rope down there." He helped Tom stand the alien up. The grey creature was calm, showing no aggression towards his captors. "You're going to take that thing downstairs? There's kids down there!" Daphne protested. Thunder boomed outdoors. Nathan and Tom began to escort the life-form across the kitchen. " But this is a real alien," Nathan said in awe, "We're not alone anymore, this guy proves I saw an alien ship destroy the city. I say we learn what we can about it while it's alive. We don't even know if we can kill it." Tom chimed in, "We can. This ain't the only one I shot, I got them other ones with a clean shot to the head. Trust me, they can't survive that." Daphne glanced down at her man knocked out on the floor. "What about Scott?" Daphne exclaimed as the men forced the alien down the basement staircase. Nathan called back to his friend, "Don't worry Daphne, I'm sure he's having sweet dreams." Scott was in fact having the wildest dreams of his life.

In the world of Scott's dream he was a child again, living his earliest memories. He knew he was supposed to be an adult but the hands and body of a child felt fitting for him. It was all so familiar, his childhood home and the enchantment of a sunset in your youth. Scott was in his backyard chasing his childhood dog. Scott's brother was there with him in the dream. Strangely enough in the dream Scott's brother's name was Paragon. He didn't look like himself though. Paragon had a bald head and grey skin. Something inside Paragon's presence allowed Scott to identify him. The next thing Scott knew he was in his room saying his nightly prayers with his father. He shared a bed with his brother, who still looked alien to him. Scott asked why he looked the way he did, but his brother only stared back. Scott knew that without a nose his brother Paragon breathed through the pores in his face and head. Paragon's ears weren't necessary either as he could hear Scott through the same pores he breathed. Scott was fascinated by how much he was learning about his brother just by being around him. Scott's hand traced the wall of the bathroom looking for the light switch. His hand was still childlike and he had to reach up to find his target. The wall however felt strange. The painted texture of the surface instead felt like cold metal. Scott found the light but the bathroom looked like nothing he had ever seen in his life. He wasn't even sure he could call it a bathroom. Suddenly he was washing his little hands, unable to shut off the confusing water faucets. He struggled turning the alien knobs as his wet fingers gripped them tight. After a while his father appeared. He recognized the warmth of his father, who looked younger and sported a dark beard. Scott watched his father effortlessly shut off the running water. His father grabbed him by the hand and walked him back to bed. Scott held on tight to his father's grey three fingered hand. He looked up to see his dad in the darkness, standing bald and grey. Thunder roared outside as Scott stood with his high school classmates. All the kids were there in their graduation gowns ready to walk across the stage. They were all on their school football field for the ceremony. Scott looked up at the crowds of family who had gathered. Scott's eyes scanned through the grey faces in the crowd until he recognized his family. His mom's dark hair worn up off her neck with his dad's long grey arm draped around her. Scott took to the stage and shook hands with a grey figure, his principal, and accepted his diploma. Scott was happy to graduate from Paragon Public schools.

Back inside the Bolton's underground shelter Tom and Craig were tying the alien to a chair. Daphne was getting the cot ready while Nathan and his father carried Scott over to rest. Mrs. Bolton was trying to salvage the dinner she had prepared and did her best to avoid the creature. Craig's two children watched as their father tied up the alien. A purring like noise came from the alien as his body vibrated in rhythm. "Is that thing a cat?" Craig's young daughter Sarah asked. Her brother Cj scoffed at her and remarked, "some cat, that's a spaceman!" He leaned in to look Closer at the alien. It's soft purr turned back into the screech it made earlier. "Can we shut this thing up?" Craig asked as Tom wrapped the ropes tight Around the alien. Tom shook his head as the whistling scream scared off the small children. Once they were out of the aliens presence the whistling subsided. The Bolton's positioned Scott so that he would be comfortable and left him in Daphne's care.

Scott continued to dream. This time he was flying over the countryside. The ship he was in was unlike anything Scott had ever seen. It was the largest thing Scott had ever been a part of. It's shape resembled a stingray swimming in water. There were hundreds of legs on the bottom of the ship, anchoring it to the planet below. The legs resembled the roots of a plant. It was piloted by thousands of crewmen that he worked alongside. They were carrying thousands more with them. Their purpose wasn't clear but Scott followed his duties. His grey body and the thousands beside him were mentally linked to the ship. Together they piloted this behemoth. He dreamed about his daily routine on the ship and how it had led them here across a vast ocean of darkness. Scott didn't recognize where he was but he was not on Earth. Dark clouds formed around his ship as bolts of lightning crackled outside. The storm provided camouflage and energy as lightning danced along the ship's surface. Somehow the ship was feeding on the electricity the storm provided. His fellow crewmen were both human and grey aliens. Scott found himself working alongside Javier and Ben, to his delight. It was very familiar to be back with them. They even shared in smoking a joint Scott had rolled for the occasion. Their ship had arrived at the destination, Scott turned to celebrate with his friends. Javier and Ben were dead on the floor. Scott tried to wake them up but it was no good. Daphne approached Scott out of nowhere and reached out. Scott's hand held onto her soft hand as she led him through the darkness. They were back in Scott's apartment, in bed. Daphne was on top of Scott kissing him. Her blonde hair fell around his face as she kissed his neck. Scott's eyes closed as her lips nibbled his neck. When he opened his eyes he saw Daphne on top of him, only she was a grey alien. Scott wrapped his arm around her waist and flipped Daphne over to be on top of her. It wasn't long before Scott was back at Paragon Car wash. His three fingered grey hand guided a small sedan in for a wash. Javier and Ben came running into the car wash on fire. Scott was panicking as his coworkers yelled about an invasion. Scott looked outside the car wash to see a small ship crash. Several humans emerged from inside and began to look around. Scott hid from the humans as their appearance frightened him. He hid in the basement, only it was Bolton's basement. Above him he could hear footsteps as they grew closer. The door to the basement swung open and at the top of the stairs stood an alien. Scott's grey body trembled as the alien Approached. Two hands gripped Scott's shoulders, yanking him to his feet. He looked up at the alien, with it's dark brown hair and blue eyes. Scott knew he was staring into his own reflection. He was an alien. Scott's vision of himself yelled out, "Paragon!" the one word echoed in Scott's head as the vision of himself faded. With each echo Scott felt himself falling. The word Paragon became physical glass he would shatter as he descended further. When the falling stopped Scott found himself in his backyard still chasing his dog. Scott's dream repeated itself over and over in its entirety.

Chapter Nine

KELLY MILLER HAD BEEN SPENDING LESS TIME WITH HER HUSBAND since arriving at Landry. Her time had been occupied at the side of her friend Dana Webb. Kelly felt as if she were Dana's assistant with the amount of mundane tasks assigned to her. It began as little things, collecting coffee or dropping laundry at the facilities. Kelly was desperate to talk to her husband Ben about their stay at Landry. They were told that the world was ending, and that there was not much of a world left to return to but Kelly was uncertain. It could not be over in that short amount of time, could it? Was it four days? Or even five days that they had been underground left to wonder. The days had been running together for Kelly as she woke late in the morning to an empty room. Kelly was not surprised by Ben's absence but it was strange that their dog Kota would be missing as well. In one motion Kelly was on her feet and making her way towards the closet. Throwing on a long red cardigan she made her way to the front. In the halls outside Kelly could hear her neighbors arguing through their door. She smirked to herself as she realized she had gone out without spending any time on her hygiene. This was serious, as a dog mom Kelly knew something was up. Ben was not known for taking Kota to work, and knowing him he was undoubtedly hours into his work day.

There was a chill in the air in the hallways of Landry as Kelly continued to search for Kota. After a few minutes she came across another woman and her daughter also searching for their dog. Kelly saw the panic in the little girl's eyes and wanted to help search with them. As she turned back to confront the pair an explosion echoed above and knocked the lights out.

Javier Rodrigues was eager to finish his morning shift in the kitchen. The weekend had passed rather quickly for Javier and his family. They kept to themselves in their room when the boys were not working. Tiago had denied Ben's work request each morning since they had arrived. Ben remained calm but persistent in his vows to get Tiago working.

Four days had passed since the death of their mother and Javier was coping the best he could. Once they had talked their father into staying through the weekend the grief had time to catch up with them. Work kept Javier distracted for a time but going back to his room brought him joy. Tiago had taken to singing again for the first time since Javier was a boy. Every afternoon before dinner he would sit and sing songs about love and about his wife. Javier was happy to have memories of his parents singing together, but David and Al could not say the same.

It was not long before Javier was off work and he made his way to the laundry rooms to collect his brother David. The two teenagers walked back to their room together without saying too much about their day. As the two of them walked a young girl and her mother approached. The daughter had tears in her eyes and asked about her missing puppy. The two boys were unable to offer her any help and they parted ways.

The Rodrigues boys made it to their rooms, but David's knock was drowned out as darkness swept over them.

Ben ran down the halls of Landry towards the main elevator. The explosion had come from that direction and sent the bunker into a panicked state. Everyone was outside of their rooms and in the darkened halls which made it difficult for Ben to catch up to T and Matt. The two brothers had gotten a head start for the elevator but Ben was in pursuit. Luckily for Ben he still carried his personal keys and had a flashlight key-chain to aid him. The smoke was limiting Ben's view in the hall as he approached the elevator. It was too quiet considering Matt and T should have arrived by now. Ben was cautious as he glanced inside. He shined his light on the doors, which looked as if they had been melted despite being cold to the touch. The elevator was empty, the ceiling too melted and collapsed. Ben had no doubt that the explosion came from the falling elevator. From what Ben could see, the cables had been cut from whatever melted through the door.

Footsteps crept up behind Ben as his body swiveled to shine his light on what lurked. Nothing. As Ben's light shined through the smoke he began to hear the whispers of someone crying out. Ben shined his light to his left and saw T on the ground. It was dark even with the light but Ben could tell that blood pooled around the man on the ground. As Ben approached T's eyes got wide as he began to cry out, unable to put together a distinguishable word. "What happened?" Ben pleaded as he saw how bad T's condition was. Half of T's body was burned, and his face and neck had gashes exposing muscle and bone. T was unable to speak as he motioned for his gun on the floor. Ben picked the gun up reluctantly as he remembered his own holstered weapon. "We're.." T"s struggling voice was alarming, "Not, alone." T's words were followed by a cough as blood spit out from his lips.

Is someone here? Ben thought to himself. Before Ben could stand he felt a chilling breath on the back of his neck.

Chapter Ten

JAVIER AND HIS BROTHERS HUDDLED WITH THEIR FATHER IN THE dark. Gunfire erupted down the halls outside as the four men held each other close within the walls of their room.

Ben Miller was not going to be overpowered by his assailant.

This thing is not human! Ben's mind raced as he scrambled to get a shot at the alien before him. The creature was agile and evaded round after round by jumping to the ceiling. Ben was not prepared for that and felt a chill run up his spine as he tried to remain calm. The grey skin of the creature was wet with red blood from the brothers it had killed. Ben planted his feet, aiming his handgun toward the creature. It whistled it's haunting scream. As Ben lost his composure and shielded his ears the grey alien lunged for him. As the two fell to the ground in the dark Ben lost his gun. The fall had broken his flashlight and he was alone in the dark against this alien creature on top of him. Ben knew he could be killed any time by this thing and did all he could, headbutting the alien above. The alien staggered backwards off of Ben's body as he sprang to his feet. On equal footing Ben had height to his advantage. The creature shook its head as its wide eyes blinked. Ben's holstered sidearm was still an option, having lost T's weapon during the fall. Adrenaline fueled his actions as Ben's hands wrapped around the alien's neck. The alien's feet kicked in the air as Ben lifted it from the ground. The alien squirmed in his hands as Ben effortlessly lifted it up over his own head. This thing is light, He thought. The aliens body twitched as it tried to hold onto his arms. A choking cough erupted before it let out another horrific scream. Ben tightened his grip until the weakened cries silenced and the crack of the alien's neck brought its end. Ben dropped the body to the ground and his knees buckled. Catching himself before the fall Ben regained himself. He had never killed anything like that before. As Ben scrambled away from the elevator and death he wanted desperately to be with Kelly.

Half an hour passed in the bunker as Kelly and Ben talked about what happened. She did her best to comfort her shaken husband and to listen to him ramble about killing the alien creature. Ben was expecting the knock that came on their door as Kelly left his side. She returned into the candle lit room accompanied by Mr. Webb. His demeanor was far more serious than usual. "Ben, first off, are you okay son?" Mr. Webb asked, to which Ben nodded. "When it all happened my daughter and I took shelter in our rooms. Once the commotion stopped I gathered myself to come find you. I had no doubt you would have firsthand knowledge, so what was it?" Mr. Webb's intrigue and fear echoed in his tone. "Well, for starters we have three dead bodies to clean up by the elevator," Ben's voice was faint. The young man's throat felt dry saying it. Mr. Webb's shock washed over his face, "What? Who is it?" The older man asked as candle flames danced wildly in the darkness. "No one mentioned aliens when they said the world was ending, sir," Ben continued, "Matt and his brother T are dead. They were killed by the alien that destroyed our elevator." Ben stood up to face Mr. Webb as Kelly listened to the interaction. Mr. Webb turned away from them and remained silent for a moment before he spoke. "Here's what I'd like you to do Ben," Mr. Webb's voice was low as he kept his back to them, "I want you to get a small crew together. Go collect the bodies. take them somewhere they won't be seen. As for the elevator," Mr. Webb turned to face them. He seemed to be piecing his plan together as he talked, "Don't we have Javier and his family staying with us? Now would be the time to put his father to work," Mr. Webb's eyes followed a candle flame as it rocked back and forth. "I'll leave you to it Benjamin." Ben nodded as Mr. Webb turned for the door. "Oh and let's keep this alien thing quiet as best we can," Mr. Webb said as he reached the door. "We don't want to cause any extra panic down here," he chuckled. Mr. Webb showed himself out as Kelly got up from her seat to lock the door behind him. "Are we safe down here?" Kelly asked her husband as she entered into his arms. As the couple stood in each other's embrace Ben tried to comfort her, "Safer than with the aliens up there." Her arms wrapped tight around him as remorse fell over Ben. Last night he had sacrificed Kota's spot in the bunker along with the other pets to keep Mr. Webb satisfied. Ben told himself that despite knowing what he knew now it was still for the best if it kept Kelly safe.

Later that night in the Rodrigues room Ben tried to convince Tiago to work within the walls of Landry. "The answer is no," Tiago declared as he sat across from Ben at the table. Javier watched as his father and former manager went back and forth. David and Al were quiet beside him on the bed. "Please, Mr. Rodrigues," Ben continued, "We just need you to take a look at our main elevator door. We had a malfunction tonight and-" Tiago scoffed, interrupting Ben. "What malfunctioning elevator sounds like a war zone?" Tiago's eyebrow raised as he asked. Ben sighed, "Look," His eyes scanned the room, specifically to Javier and his brothers. Ben's eyes met with Tiago's stare, "Trust me you do not want to be outside this bunker right now. But if you don't work with us then that could become a possibility for you and your sons." Tiago looked to his boys and replied, "We just lost my wife, so forgive me if I'm going to say no so that I may grieve in peace." Ben did not look away from Tiago. "Mr. Webb won't like hearing you decline, please reconsider for your son's sake," Ben stood as Tiago joined him. "Tell your boss that we are thankful to be here but if we must leave then so be it," Tiago sighed and raised a hand to Ben. The younger man hesitated before shaking hands over it. Ben felt conflicted about keeping the aliens a secret from the family. Mr. Webb had given him orders and he did not want to scare Javier's young brothers. Still he struggled with his thoughts on whether he did the right thing as he left to report to Mr. Webb.

Once Ben was gone Tiago locked the door and turned to his sons declaring, "This settles it boys, we're leaving tonight."

In Mr. Webb's Office Ben informed his boss of his failed attempt to convince Tiago Rodrigues. Mr. Webb's chair squeaked as he turned to face the candles arranged on his desk. "Ben, tonight at midnight you are going visit the Rodrigues family," Mr. Webb's words were firm. "Without power we won't last another twenty four hours, and that man is being selfish to refuse us our survival." Ben blinked as he remained silent. Mr. Webb continued, "We'll get him to work by force if we have to." Ben nodded as Mr. Webb continued, "it would be in everyone's best interests to get that elevator sealed. If anymore of those aliens make it down here we could be done for." Mr. Webb's words worried Ben, who replied, "Is that a good idea sir?" Mr. Webb's demeanor changed as Ben expressed his concerns, "Won't we be locking ourselves down here?" Ben knew he had to ask these questions now for the sake of everyone who did not have a voice. "Ben, you let me worry about that," Mr. Webb exclaimed, "We built an escape tunnel for these situations." Mr. Webb and Ben had softened their guard with one another, so Ben asked, "And where is this tunnel?" Mr. Webb leaned back into his chair as he pulled open a drawer from his desk. He pulled out his key-card, "It's locked in here with us," Mr. Webb chuckled. Behind the old man's desk there was an empty fireplace. Mr. Webb stood and approached it with his key-card. Placing the card to the inactive panel Mr. Webb looked to Ben and spoke, "The truth is, without that man's help, We're trapped down here. No way out, with one way in for the aliens." Ben felt a lump in his throat.

Chapter Eleven

SCOTT'S HEAD POUNDED AS HE REGAINED CONSCIOUSNESS. IT FELT like he had been awake for hours but unable to open his eyes or move. His head was groggy as he heard the echo of people talking not far from him.

As Scott sat up he realized he was not alone. Sitting across from him in a chair was Craig Callahan's young son Cj. "That alien fucked you up," Cj barked as he leapt out of his seat. Scott stood on weak legs, "should you be talking like that? What are you six?" Scott snarked at the kid as he made his way to the door. "Eight! Why does everyone think I'm a little kid!" Cj cried out behind Scott. The smell of food cooking in the kitchen brought Scott back to life. Mrs. Bolton was hard at work with the help of Cj's little sister. Craig, Cj and Sarah's father, was at the table with Mr. Bolton and their friend Tom. "Oh, that's a lovely name dear," Mrs. Bolton could be heard from the kitchen. Craig's daughter Sarah was beside the Bolton matriarch. At the same time the men seated around the table erupted in laughter over their game of cards. Sarah ran off from the kitchen leaving Mrs. Bolton alone as Scott greeted everyone. "We thought you might be gone," Mr. Bolton chuckled as he stood to shake Scott's hand, saying, "Good to see you on your feet, son." Scott looked around before he asked, "Where is Daphne?"

Nathan Bolton and Daphne Williams had been alternating shifts guarding the home. Over the weekend they had managed to kill three more aliens approaching the house. The storm outside had not stopped and it limited their view of the outside world. The days were dark as night and the aliens moved like shadows outside the Bolton home. One was no physical match, but if they came in numbers, Daphne feared they could take the house. Luckily they had remained undetected as long as they had. Daphne sat on the back patio as Scott approached her. "Hello beautiful," He said as Daphne turned smiling at him. She was in his arms in an instant and happy to know he had recovered. "We were all worried about you," Daphne said as they kissed. "I have to tell you something," Scott said as they held each other. "It's about this dream I had," He spoke as Daphne looked up into his eyes. She nodded and replied, "I have a lot you need to hear, too."

Nathan was ready for some of his mother's delicious home cooking. The world had turned crazy but he could depend on her for a hot meal. Before dinner he wanted to go and check on their prisoner. Mr. Bolton and Daphne decided to keep the alien through the weekend. They moved their alien prisoner upstairs into Nathan's bedroom. Mrs. Bolton immediately insisted on making meals for the alien upstairs. At first everyone was reluctant to feed it, but Mrs. Bolton vowed to go if no one else would. Nathan would not risk his mother going near that thing and found himself catering to an alien in his own home. As Nathan made it upstairs he thought about all the years running up and down those stairs. He had called this place home for all his life and now everything felt out of place. Cold beads of sweat ran down Nathan's neck as he discovered his bedroom door cracked open. He sat down the plate he was carrying and slowly grabbed the bedroom doorknob. The door flew open as he lunged inside to find the alien squatting on a chair. Sarah Callahan was inside the room and did not seem to be scared. She stood a few feet from the alien and looked embarrassed to be caught. "What the hell are you doing?" Nathan barked as the child ran past him out of the room.

You better run, Nathan thought to himself. The young man had spent so much time in his bedroom growing up that every detail stood out. His frustration prevented him from noticing the open bedroom window behind him. Nathan turned back to the grey skinned alien that was now on its feet as the bedroom door closed. Crawling on the ceiling above Nathan were two more aliens. The three creatures were in an aggressive stance. Together they let out their haunting scream before attacking.

Scott felt relieved to know that the alien was alive. After his dream Scott's opinion about the creature was a blur. Daphne filled him in on how they had kept it upstairs and their shifts to watch the house and the alien. Scott began explaining his dream to Daphne as the menacing cries broke out upstairs.

Nathan's fight with the aliens dragged out across his bedroom. they lunged for him in unison, tackling Nathan onto the bed. Adrenaline kicked in as Nathan threw one of the grey aliens off in defense. The agile alien recovered quickly as it darted back to attack. Nathan blocked the swings of another alien as the last grey put its finger in his eye. The alien pressed into Nathan's eye socket causing him to cry out. Nathan put his own thumb into the aliens left eye and drove it straight in. His human hand was smaller than the grey aliens' own appendage. This was also the case for their eyes, which allowed Nathan's thumb to get in deep. The pressure was off of Nathan as the alien fell back crying out in pain. Nathan stood up on the bed and kicked the blinded alien in the right temple. The creature's skull caved in on impact and the body fell to the floor as it twitched clinging to life. The other two aliens cried again. Before they could attack Nathan a shot rang out with one alien on the receiving end. Two bodies laid on the floor as Daphne aimed her gun at the last remaining alien. Scott stood frozen behind her as the rest of the bunker residents looked on from the hall. "Kill it," Nathan yelled. Scott felt connected to this alien, it was the one he had touched.

He managed to survive through all this? Scott thought about the alien as Daphne lowered her gun. "No," She declared, "We agreed to keep one alive, remember?" At this time Mrs. Bolton had pushed her way to be next to Scott, "My son," She spoke under her breath. "Look what that got us," Nathan countered to Daphne as the young girl Sarah returned to the room. "Edgar, are you hurt?" Sarah yelled to the alien as she ran to it. Craig Callahan shouted from the hall for his daughter but it did not stop her. Scott stepped forward but Mrs. Bolton grabbed his wrist stopping him. Daphne called for the little girl, "Sarah, sweetie, what did you call that thing?" She questioned the child. Nathan scoffed. "We named him Edgar, since he's going to be staying with us," Sarah said as she smiled at the grey skinned alien. "Sarah! Honey- please get away from that thing!" Craig yelled from behind Scott. "Daphne grab her," Craig pleaded. Daphne stepped forward to collect Sarah and as she grabbed the young girl the alien screamed. The alien pulled on Sarah's free arm as its scream frightened everyone. In a quick motion Nathan was on the alien and had it in a chokehold.

Scott fell to his knees in pain as he watched life escape the alien named Edgar. Scott had known Edgar their entire lives up until this point because of whatever Edgar's touch did to him. At the same time Sarah screamed from Daphne's arms as she ran out of the room. Mrs. Bolton cried out as well, not for her son, but in opposition. "Stupid boy, what have you done?" She cried as Nathan dropped the body. "Mom?" Nathan cried, shocked to hear his mother talk to him that way. "Mom it was dangerous to keep that thing here," Nathan said as he put his hand on his mothers shoulder. She shrugged him off as tears ran down her face. "You killed my boy you stupid mother-fucker!" she screamed in her son's face. Scott knew what was happening. Edgar and his people had numerous gifts. Not only could they pass knowledge through contact, as in Scott's case, they could also bond minds. That bond could be described as a blinding intense love unlike any other. "Now Connie," Mr. Bolton stepped in to calm his wife. As Mr. Bolton stepped in Nathan went to Scott to help him to his feet. "Listen to yourself." Mr. Bolton pleaded, throwing himself around his wife to comfort her. "Calm down, that's our Nathan," Mr. Bolton assured her. He hardly recognized his wife in his arms as she fired back, "That's no son of mine!" as she reached down to Mr. Bolton's waist and plucked his pocket knife from him. Scott had barely made it to his feet as warm blood splattered on his face. Nathan screamed in pain as his mother drove a knife into his right shoulder from behind. "NO!" Mr. Bolton cried as his wife stabbed their son a second time. "No son of mine!" She yelled as Nathan went to the floor. Scott's tears ran down his face as Nathan looked up at him in pain. The third strike landed in Nathan's chest as his blood spilled into his lungs. Mr. Bolton pulled his wife off of their bloodied son as she swung the blade wildly. He overpowered her and forced her to drop the knife as they went to the floor. Daphne placed pillows behind Nathan's head while Scott applied pressure to his wounds. Tom and Craig pulled Mrs. Bolton from the floor and then helped Mr. Bolton to his feet. The two men escorted a screaming Mrs. Bolton out of the room as her husband sat with their son. He couldn't imagine seeing his boy like this, let alone his wife being the perpetrator. For the first and last time in his life Nathan Bolton saw his father cry.

Chapter Twelve

KELLY MILLER WAS SUSPICIOUS OF HER HUSBAND BEN. AFTER dinner he left her alone with Dana Webb and she had been trying to lose her friend ever since. A few bottles of wine into their night and Kelly had Dana where she wanted her, in a drunken slumber. Kelly left Dana's room quietly in the night and made her way down the dark hall to her own room. She was hoping to find Ben in their room but instead ran into more than she expected on her way there.

Javier Rodrigues and his brothers were ready to leave with their father when Ben knocked on the door. He was armed and had two men with him. "We're not asking nicely," Ben informed Tiago. "You will shoot me if I don't work for you?" Tiago challenged Ben's now drawn sidearm. "It doesn't have to be you. There are four of you," Ben's words were cold, and Javier grew angry hearing him. "Has it really come to this then?" Tiago's voice was defeated. "Perhaps I was being stubborn, but you Ben, have become something else," Tiago sighed as he looked at his sons. Javier gave his father a nod. "Take care of them," Tiago said to Javier. Ben motioned Tiago for the door, stating, "Get your work done and you can come back to them. Misbehave and I decide what to do with you." Ben's voice was commanding. "You really think you're in control huh?" Javier shouted with anger and disappointment in his voice. Ben smiled from the doorway, "Something like that," he remarked. The Rodrigues boys were quiet as the three armed men escorted their father out. As David closed the door someone reached out, holding the door open. David jumped back startled as Kelly Miller emerged to say, "It's okay, I heard the whole thing boys."

"What do you expect me to do at this time of night?" Tiago asked. Ben was in his thoughts. He was playing the bad guy role to get help for everybody inside the bunker. *Why don't you just be honest?* Ben thought. "We need to figure out how to get the electric back on. Then you need to figure out what to do about this," Ben said as his flashlight shined ahead to the scene at the elevator. "We have to do something about these doors by morning," Ben demanded. *Or who knows what could happen,* he thought to himself. Tiago had a long night ahead of him, and Ben would be looking over his shoulder every minute.

"So you were planning an escape tonight?" Kelly asked Javier as he stared into her eyes. She had talked with him from time to time at Paragon Car Wash while visiting Ben, and knew about his crush. She would use that to her advantage tonight. "My husband thinks it's safe for us to stay down here, but we're sardines packed in a can for what's outside," Kelly ranted. David and Al fought over who would sit in the free chair at the table. David won. "What's out there?" Al asked from the floor. Kelly's eyes were kind. She knew this was life changing news but these young boys would find out sooner or later. "We're dealing with a possible alien invasion," Kelly confessed, although she felt weird saying it. "Aliens?" Javier asked, "Like the little green kind?" His confusion was matched by his two brothers. "Yeah, well something like that. I want to get out and find somewhere we can really be safe." Kelly replied. Her attitude calmed the boys. "Are you with me?" she asked. Javier looked at his brothers and they all agreed.

Daphne and Scott went outside to watch the rain. They had not said much to each other since Nathan died, but they held hands in silence. Mrs. Bolton was locked upstairs away from everyone. Mr. Bolton was with Tom and Craig, who were doing their best to get him drunk and comfort him. "I hope my dad is okay," Daphne said over the rain. Scott put his arm around her. "That's a shitty thing to say when my friend just died, but I hope Dad's okay," She cried. Scott held his girlfriend in his arms, but his mind was on his dream from before. All the things he saw and Javier and Ben. "Let's go back," Scott declared, "Let's go to your dad's and get him and then head back home. We don't have anything here and the aliens are moving away from the city." Scott's words sparked Daphne's curiosity as she replied, "How do you know the aliens are leaving the cities?" Scott held Daphne's hand and told her everything about his dream and his connection to the aliens. "Well if what you say is true, I'll follow you wherever you want to go," Daphne replied. "Like you said," Daphne finished, "There's no reason to stay here." Daphne's words gave her a new resolve as she wiped away tears.

Scott pulled a pre-rolled joint from his pocket and lit it. "For Nathan," Scott said between puffs. Daphne took a hit, "For Nathan," She stated before a long drag. The smoke she exhaled lingered around them for a moment before drifting into the rain.

After their smoke the couple went inside to pack. Scott was able to convince Tom and Craig to come with them, and the three men went to confront Mr. Bolton. "Let me do the talking," Tom declared in the hall, "I've known him the longest." Tom led the way into Mr. Bolton's room. "Hey-" Tom began but Scott cut him off declaring, "Mr. Bolton, we're heading back to the city. I'm sorry about Nathan but-" Before Scott could finish Mr. Bolton was standing ready. "I don't ever want to see this house again," He blurted out. "What about your wife?" Craig asked. Mr. Bolton went to his closet to fetch his coat. "I'll talk to her," The man replied. They left him alone while they collected their things downstairs.

Daphne, Scott, Tom, Craig and his children all loaded up their things into Nathan's truck. Scott suggested taking Daphne's car but she declined. Her car would not make the trip with the remaining fuel it had. A single gunshot echoed from the house as everyone looked at one another. A moment of silence passed as Mr. Bolton emerged out the front door without ever looking back. "Let's go while there's daylight," He ordered as he jumped in his son's truck. The sky was still dark as the truck's tires kicked up mud and rain. The road was empty as Tom focused on driving, Mr. Bolton sat quietly beside him. Daphne was eager to get back to her father's house as they approached his driveway. Headlights pierced the night to reveal the smoldering remains of Jim Williams' home. The embers were still red hot despite the pouring rain.

Chapter Thirteen

TIAGO WORKED DILIGENTLY TO GET THE BACK UP GENERATORS going for the people of Landry. The residents would wake up to a normal day in the bunker thanks to him. Unfortunately for Tiago his work day had no end in sight as Ben insisted he continue. Mr. Webb made it clear that Ben was to keep Tiago busy until the main elevator was secured. Not long after they began their work Tiago and Ben began to hear shouts, "Aliens! We're under attack!"

Meanwhile Kelly Miller had gone back to her room in the night to pack her things. She was leaving tonight with Javier and his brothers, once they had what they needed. Kelly was all set when she had a knock at her door. She was expecting Javier or his brothers but instead Dana Webb stood in the hall. "Where did you go?" Dana cried in a drunken voice. Sleep had not been kind to her as she pushed her way into Kelly's room. "I went, home. Obviously," Kelly sighed as she shut the door behind her. Dana sprawled out on the bed. She was still wearing her clothes from that day and had her shoes on the bed. Kelly did not have time for this. "Dana," She demanded, "You need to get some rest, sleep it off here tonight." Kelly removed Dana's shoes for her as Dana squirmed. "Stop," Dana laughed. Kelly stepped away from her friend on the bed, she needed to be somewhere. As Kelly grabbed one of her bags the lights came back on. *I guess their dad did it,* Kelly thought to herself. Dana shielded her eyes from the light before noticing Kelly. Sitting up quickly as Kelly began to walk to the door Dana shouted, "Stop." Kelly rolled her eyes as she stopped and turned back to her drunk friend, "What now?" She questioned. Dana giggled to herself before reaching into the back of her waistband. "Shhh," Dana laughed, "I took this from daddy today." Dana revealed a small snub nosed revolver. "Jeez, Dana!" Kelly shouted as Dana pointed it at her. "N-No, it's cool," Dana said as she lowered the gun, "I'm saving you, take it." Dana giggled as she extended the gun out. Her finger and her thumb pinched the barrel as if it were infectious as Kelly collected the weapon. "Uhm-yeah, okay," Kelly sighed with relief as she spoke. *Maybe I did have time for this,* she thought as she put the gun away. It was a few inches long, and held five bullets. Kelly hoped she would not have to fire a single one. Dana leaned back on the bed and got comfortable. A minute after Dana shut her eyes Kelly was in the hall with her bags.

Javier Rodrigues waited with his brothers until the power was restored. Once they were good to go Javier led his brothers down the hallways and knocked on every door they passed. With every door they knocked on they continued shouting "Aliens! We're under attack!" They led a large following in the halls, carrying on the shouts, "Aliens! We're under attack!" culminating as a chant as their numbers grew. Kelly Miller smiled at Javier as she joined them. Javier felt accomplished to be rallying everyone like this with his brothers. They marched as a group to the main elevator. Ben had his gun drawn and was on alert as their chant quieted. "What the hell is this?" Ben shouted as he lowered his weapon into its holster. Tiago stepped out from behind Ben and looked at his boys, "Did you do this?" He asked. David shouted, "Let my dad go!" As the gathered crowd mumbled. "Ben," Kelly said as she stepped forward, "You've gotten out of hand," She pleaded as she approached her husband. "We want answers!" Someone cried out from the crowd. "Honey," Kelly spoke softly, "Don't be like Mr. Webb, help these people." The crowd shouted their desires for answers as Ben and Kelly held hands. As the volume picked up a gunshot rangout. Mr. Webb stood in the back of the crowd with a smoking gun raised to the ceiling. "That is enough!" He shouted. "You people wouldn't even have this place if my contractors hadn't built it," Mr. Webb cried as he lowered his weapon. "Look around, you won't see any of them here to enjoy it," Mr. Webb said as he spat on the ground. The two men that had accompanied Ben earlier were present backing Mr. Webb. Ben had a bad feeling in his gut. Mr. Webb made his way to the front, standing between Ben and the crowd. Kelly squeezed Ben's hand as Mr. Webb began to speak again. "If you people want to have rooms to go back to," He shouted, "I suggest you let these men work." The crowd grew quiet as Mr. Webb's armed men stood by. Javier's forehead had beads of sweat running into his eyes as his father stepped forward. Tiago's voice was loud and stern, "I will not work for you," He commanded. Mr. Webb's face grew angry. *You're making this hard on yourself,* Ben thought as he watched. "Perhaps if you had allowed one of those contractors to come, then you would not be so dependent on me," Tiago argued. Mr. Webb's anger swelled. He could not stand to be insulted like that and drew his gun. Al cried out as he held onto his eldest brother. "Mr. Webb," Ben pleaded, hoping to de-escalate things. "We can-'' Ben tried to talk as Mr. Webb cut him off. "No, either Mr. Rodrigues here gets back to work or he takes his chances up top with who knows what!" Javier's heart pounded as he watched his father face down the barrel of Mr. Webb's gun. Tiago stood firm replying, "Thank you for taking my family in, but my son's and I will be leaving." Tiago looked over to his son's with pride and a smile on his face. A gunshot echoed as Javier closed his eyes and held his brother. The crowd began to scream in terror as a second alien emerged from the melted elevator doorway. Tiago ran to his son's as Kelly pulled back the hammer on her gun. She was the first to notice the grey alien while everything was going on. *One down, four bullets left,* Kelly noted to herself. As the second alien climbed out passing Kelly's first kill it Whistled it's haunting scream. Behind it emerged two more grey creatures, as more whistled from the elevator shaft above. The crowd was panicking and scattering through the halls. Ben, Kelly, Mr. Webb and his guards all opened fire on the creatures crawling out. They had killed eight in total before they stopped coming. *Two bullets left,* Kelly worried as she looked to her husband. "Your office, sir," Ben said to Mr. Webb as he pulled out his key card. "I'll lead the way," Webb replied. Javier and his family were huddled in each other's arms as Kelly and Ben darted by them in the hall. "Javier!" Kelly shouted as she slowed. "Guy's, let's get going!" Ben shouted to the family. David and Al led the way as Javier and Tiago took up the rear. People scrambled to get to their rooms to get any personal possessions they could carry. The majority of Landry's residents rushed to Mr. Webb's office. "Move out of the way people," Mr. Webb shouted as he pushed to his own door. "You have nowhere to go without me after-all," He boasted as his key card opened his office to the public. Inside the office Mr. Webb wasted no time activating the backdoor in his fireplace. The magnetized door swung open revealing a metal ladder leading out. "After me everyone," Mr. Webb declared. As he grabbed the ladder Ben stopped him. "Not so fast sir," Ben insisted, gun drawn. Mr. Webb looked back at him alarmed, "Really Ben, you pick a time like this to grow a spine?" Mr. Webb scoffed as Ben remained silent while raising the gun further. "You go last," Ben threatened.

Chapter Fourteen

"You have to be compatible with the Grey's in order to be influenced by them," Scott choked on his words. Smoke lingered around him in the crowded vehicle. "I wish you wouldn't smoke in the car with my kids," Craig Callahan remarked. Sarah was quietly sitting in Daphne's lap as Cj sat with their father. Scott waved his hand through the air while Tom sat in front of him in the driver seat. "I Don't mind dad," Cj said while tilting his head back to see his father. "Yes you do, son," Craig insisted. Daphne sat in the middle of the two men in the backseat and put her hand on Scott's leg. "Maybe you should put it out until we get there?" She asked before continuing, "How much did you bring with you anyway?" Mr. Bolton broke his silence since they'd left to chuckle at the question. "Enough," Scott said as he smiled before taking a drag. Scott reached up to the window with his joint knocking the ember off in the wind. Mr. Bolton had been silent until now, "Scott, let me hit that before you put it out." Craig scoffed as Daphne passed the joint between her boyfriend and Mr. Bolton. Tom laughed from the driver seat, commenting, "I wouldn't count on getting that back." Mr. Bolton enjoyed his smoke while Daphne asked, "So what else do you know about these things?" Scott looked at the kids in the backseat and up to his girlfriend. Her face had inexplicably lost its appeal since the last time he had really looked at her. Or perhaps he had not really looked at her at all since the alien crossed minds with him. "Oh my god," Tom cried from the front seat as he slowed the truck to a stop. Ahead of them in the road stood a large metallic structure. The rain was blinding but it was unmistakable. The metal was twenty to thirty feet wide in diameter and stretched to the clouds. Lightning in the sky flickered around the body that stood on multiple legs like the one in front of them. "That's a ship," Scott remarked as he gazed at it in person. He had only ever dreamed of one like this. "A spaceship?" Cj asked with intrigue. The car remained parked in the road as the rainfall engulfed them. "Not a spaceship, that one is much bigger," Scott replied, his voice filled with excitement. "They came in one ship?" Daphne asked. Scott nodded, adding, "Yes, and then that ship becomes many ships like this one." Scott stared back at the marvel in front of them. "So what is this one?" Mr. Bolton questioned. Scott smiled, "A harvester ship."

Most of the tenants of Landry had made their way up the ladder as Javier and his family ascended. The passage was narrow, Javier led the way with Tiago at the back. Javier felt a wave of curiosity come over him despite the tension. *What's on the other end of this ladder?* He thought as his hands gripped tighter. Javier reached the end of his climb as a hand pulled him up out of the shaft. He turned back to help David up, then Al. As Tiago emerged Javier looked around at the group and asked, "Where are we?" Before anyone could reply a voice answered, "None of you people are safe." Javier stepped forward and shouted, "Who said that?" A man stepped out of the dark and through the crowd. He looked familiar to Javier but through the shadows it was hard to make him out. "Hey, You're that Jerk!" Al shouted. Javier realized he was he man from their first night in Landry. If it wasn't for his mother they would not have found the bunker. "Show me some respect kid, my family built this country club on their land. I'm James Landry," he said, introducing himself.

On the other end of the ladder still in the bunker Kelly and Ben were ready to make the climb. The last person had gone and it was just them and Mr. Webb. "Wait," Donald C. Webb cried out to the couple. "Did anyone see Dana go up?" The worried father asked. Kelly cursed to herself before stating, "She must be too drunk to leave my room." Ben looked at them both, "Let's go," Ben warned his wife, "Let him go back for her." Ben grabbed his wife by the arm as Mr. Webb ran out through the office door. "We can't leave them," She cried to her husband. Kelly looked back to see Mr. Webb was gone. "I can't do this without you," Ben confessed to Kelly. They quickly kissed before Kelly made her way up the ladder with Ben close behind.

The rain continued as Nathan's truck idled in the road. "They haven't seen us yet," Tom explained, "Maybe we should go a different way?" Scott cut him off, "No, we only need to pass this ship to get where my friends are." Daphne looked at her man with concern, "Are you sure about this?" She inquired. Scott kept staring at the ship in front of them. "It hasn't made a move yet, I don't think they're interested in us," Scott said, patting Tom on the back before continuing, "Let's get going." Tom looked over to Mr. Bolton who was too high to do more than shrug. After a few seconds the truck was back in drive and on its way towards their destination. The leg of the alien ship lingered in the rearview mirror, despite the miles they put between them.

Chapter Fifteen

JAMES LANDRY HAD BEEN SURVIVING ALONE WITHIN THE WALLS OF his family's country club. As residents below were forced out Landry did his best to make them feel welcome on the surface. Most declined his offer, with one going so far as to steal supplies from him in the night.

"The grey ones aren't what you have to worry about," Landry said to the group gathered around him. Ben and Kelly were among them and Ben expressed his concern, "What do you mean?" Landry pulled back the long coat he had on to reveal his arm. As he raised his right hand it became clear to see. Just below his elbow his wrist and hand had been severed. "They don't carry weapons," Landry continued as he lowered his limb. "Instead they rely on their technology," Landry confessed. He looked to the window, stating, "It could be right outside and we'd have no way of knowing in the dark and rain." Outside of the country club lightning flashed as thunder shook the clouds.

"Technology cut off your hand?" Kelly blurted out. Landry turned back to the scared faces before him and declared, "No. I cut off my hand after it got on me. Some kind of liquid metal that's falling from the sky." Landry looked down to where his hand used to be. "It ate away at my flesh so bad that by the time I cut it off there was no blood, just dead skin and phantom pain," he sighed. The wind howled outside as the rain picked up. No one inside the country club wanted to speak. Finally Tiago Rodrigues broke the silence, "What about the elevator? We were attacked down there!" Landry sighed but before he could answer they were interrupted by the sound of a truck horn outside.

Scott was the first one out of the truck as he lit another of his joints. The rain was not going to stop him from enjoying the high. Craig insisted on staying inside the truck with his two small children. Tom and Bolton approached the main entrance of the Country Club as the doors swung open. Everyone went inside as they introduced themselves. As Scott finished his joint Javier approached. "You got any more of that?" Javier asked before hugging his friend. The two of them finished their smoke before heading in. Scott felt as though something was off. As he turned around he saw the large harvester ship from earlier slowly crawling through the sky. They were directly in its path. Scott ran to the door with Javier close behind. The large alien ship now stood at their doorstep. "Do we hide?" Someone cried out from the crowd inside. Scott and Daphne held each other close as Javier and his family stood nearby. The sound of crashing wood and debris echoed as the leg of the alien ship came down on Landry Country Club. An opening appeared at the base of the metallic leg, and hundreds of grey aliens poured out. They overran the remaining halls of Landry and in the panic Scott and Daphne were separated. It was all a blur as Scott was trampled by people helplessly running about. The grey aliens were overwhelming in number. They began pulling people in different directions and battering them with fists. Screams erupted as the building itself caught fire. Families were ripped apart amidst the chaos. Scott stood up and began to shout for Daphne but he could not see or hear her. As it all played out Scott's head began to pound. He fell to his knees as a grey alien came to his aid. Another one came to help Scott as he blacked out.

Javier and his father were on top of Al and David acting as human shields. The peoples screams were terrifying as aliens began to drag their prey back onto the ship. Javier was worried about his brothers more than anything else. A few gunshots could be heard but mostly the sounds of agony. A hand grabbed Tiago's back and pulled on him as a familiar voice pleaded with them, "We have to go!" It was Landry, who used his one arm to pull Tiago off of his son. The five of them ran to the door and made their way out. In the rain they ran from all the death and screams behind them. Javier was in the back as they were heading for the trees. He allowed himself a second to look up at the ship above them as the leg inside of the clubhouse began to retract. As it did dirt and debris flew through the air around the remains of the building. The ship above them hissed as it began to crawl again. It's distant legs would be causing the same destruction with every step it took. The trees were just ahead as Javier watched his family make it under them for safety. The rain drops that fell began to get thicker as they blurred Javier's vision. Each drop that fell on him felt heavier and warmer. His legs buckled and he slipped into the mud. Tiago turned back from under the trees and yelled, "Javi!" As Javier tried to wipe the mud and the rain from his face. As the rain and the mud began to burn around him Javier thought about what Landry had said earlier. The liquid metal that had decayed Landry's hand. Javier wiped the rain out of his face but it was like spreading hot coals. Through his blurry vision he could barely make out the blood in his palm. The pain was intense as Javier's muscles stiffened. His hearing turned to ringing as he collapsed in the rain. The mud around him was thick and made it hard to breathe as he felt the skin on his back melt. He tried as hard as he could to take a breath but the heat was in his lungs from the rain he had swallowed. His body twitched as he squirmed in the mud. He could no longer see nor hear as his body struggled. After an intense couple of minutes, Javier Rodrigues died alone in the mud.

Chapter Sixteen

SCOTT CARTER REGAINED CONSCIOUSNESS WHILE IN THE ARMS OF two grey aliens. The two dragged his body through the rubble of Landry Country Club. The leg of the alien ship was not far ahead as others were being dragged back kicking and screaming. Scott got to his feet and walked beside his alien allies through the burning remains. The fire lit their way as they approached the foot of the ship. Scott was more curious than afraid as he stepped through the membrane, entering the alien ship.

Inside the ship Scott's body and the bodies of everyone else forced aboard were encased in a metal liquid. The material was thick but still allowed them to move and breathe. It fit snug against his body, like a second layer of skin. The human screams had stopped as the metal around Scott vibrated. The leg pulsed as it lifted from the earth below. Scott and the others moved up the leg as if they were blood cells in a vein. He squirmed about as the ship constricted around his skinny body. The ship felt like a living creature, despite its liquid mercury like design. Scott and the others progressed through the ship until they found themselves in a small room. The area was open, with a ceiling a few inches above Scott's head. There were dozens of humans packed inside the small space. Scott recognized a few of them, but could not see

Daphne. She must have escaped, Scott thought. Cool metal pooled around their feet as the liquid rose up around them. Scott's body was completely engulfed. The living metal encapsulating him pulled his clothes and shoes away, dissolving them. The room drained as dozens of naked men and women huddled together. Scott covered himself with his hands as the room constricted around them. *This must be how we're transported,* Scott thought. Naked strangers pressed against Scott from all angles. They passed through the ship as if they were moving through a digestive tract. Once they came to a stop the room expanded, allowing Scott a few inches of space. The roof opened up to reveal other pods like the one they were in. There were too many to count in the dark. They could not escape, no one could. The floor began to vibrate beneath Scott's bare feet as metal wires arose. They grew from the floor like a weed towards the humans. A thick metal wire met each human as it entered their mouth and nostrils. Every orifice on their naked bodies was penetrated by the foreign metal. Scott felt a cold sensation throughout his mouth, as he took his final breath. The room filled with metal fluid once more as Scott Carter and the other's drifted out of consciousness.

When Scott came to again he was alone. He sat up on the metal structure he was stretched out on. His naked body was weak, as if he had been asleep a long time. Immediately Scott noticed that his legs and body had no hair on them. He reached to his head and felt smooth skin where his hair had been. It was dark but Scott could tell his skin was pale, almost grey. He looked around the room as he tried to stand. "Don't rush it," a calm voice spoke from the dark, alarming Scott. "Who's there?" Scott fired back as he looked about. From the darkness a small grey alien appeared. "A friend," The alien stated. Scott relaxed as he leaned back and replied, "I didn't know you people could talk." The alien smiled and approached Scott extending it's hand. Scott shook the grey alien's hand. "Thanks to the millions we collected, my species has learned your human languages. think of me as your personal Ambassador," the creature declared. As Scott and the aliens hands parted a chair formed from the ground behind the alien. The creature sat back comfortably in its metal chair. Scott smirked, "Are you controlling this place?" He asked. The alien nodded. "My species is in control," the Ambassador confirmed. Scott looked around at the metal environment. "So is this a ship we're in?" Scott asked looking up at the ceiling. The alien creature smiled, "Is that what you think we're inside right now Scott?" The alien's voice was calm. Scott looked down to meet the aliens' eyes. "How do you know my name?" Scott asked. The alien crossed its lean arms. "The same way you touched one of mine and knew about us," The Ambassador remarked. *He has a point,* Scott thought. "So, if this isn't a ship," Scott inquired, "What is it?" The Ambassador waved his hand through the air shifting the metal Scott sat on in the process. The metal sank to the floor and left Scott's naked butt on the ground. Disconnecting from the ground the metal shifted into a floating sphere in front of Scott. "This is organic, just like the two of us," The alien spoke as the metal shifted. "It exists as a microscopic life-form, my species found it in the darkness of the galaxy. It can eat a planet whole. With our genetic engineering, we can control it to terraform a planet," The grey alien stated. The metal sank to the floor. "My species has a name for it, but it would translate to Devmetal for you. For the way it devours whatever it touches," The alien remarked.

Scott watched the metal fuse back together before he spoke, "So you came to take our planet?" The alien looked Scott in the eyes and asked, "Would that matter? You know by now that you are compatible with us, that your DNA is special to my people." Scott nodded and affirmed, "I know all that, but you suggested this stuff can eat planets, is that why you wiped us out?" The grey Ambassador stood up, and walked to sit beside Scott. Being naked Scott felt uncomfortable and crossed his legs. The alien placed its left hand on Scott's thigh which caused him to scoot away. "Scott, it's not easy to tell you this, but yes. We came to take your planet," The alien confessed. He continued saying, "My people have been around for quite some time, we are older than you humans." Scott listened as the alien spoke, "We are near extinct. There were few options among the stars. We needed a compatible race to carry on our legacy," the Ambassador looked Scott in the eyes. "Your planet was abundant with life making it an easy choice to inoculate here," The alien's voice was calm. It spoke with no enthusiasm, "Your planet was rich in water. The Devmetal's solidify and die in water. There's no way they could consume the entire planet." The alien blinked as Scott stared into its wide eyes. "So," Scott questioned, "You use the Devmetal for all the dirty work and then let it die?" Scott raised a hairless eyebrow toward the Ambassador. The alien did not blink as it looked into Scott's eyes. "Long ago we bonded with the Devmetal, our living and our dead are the same," the Ambassador declared. Scott stood as he asked the alien, "What does that mean?" The ambassador patted the seat beside him signalling Scott to scoot closer. "When you have a bond like our species, you share body and mind. If you lose your mind you still have your body do you not?" The alien Ambassador asked. It raised its eyebrow imitating Scott's earlier action. Scott looked down to the floor. "You'll understand someday Scott," The Ambassador chimed in. Scott looked back to the creature and asked, "What did you need compatible humans for?" The alien leaned in close to Scott. "My species cannot reproduce on its own, Scott. we removed what's necessary for our preservation," The alien commented. Scott checked between his legs. "We left that. There were other vital reproductive organs we harvested. From you and your people," The alien assured him. Scott couldn't believe the aliens had harvested his organs like that. "There's more," The alien continued. "Taking your organs meant we had to genetically alter you. We made some modifications to the way you experience sensations. Most notable will be your sense of smell and hearing. Scott, not only are you superior to a human, you no long resemble one either," The alien declared. The Ambassador held up a piece of Devmetal. As Scott looked at the metal it became reflective. Scott hardly recognized his reflection in the mirror. He looked neither entirely human or entirely alien. He was bald with human eyes, but was missing his nose and ears like the aliens. Scott reached up to touch his face where his nose had been, then he reached for his missing ears. "You are very special, Scott Carter," the alien said as it put away the mirror. "Our Grandmaster has a plan for you," the alien stood as it spoke. "Grandmaster?" Scott asked as familiar metal probes extended from behind him. "Yes, you have been selected to carry out his will," the alien spoke with glee as Scott drifted to sleep. Scott's body had wires and probes protruding from it as a metal cocoon formed around him.

Chapter Seventeen

THE WIND WAS HOWLING AS SCOTT'S COCOON BURST OPEN IN THE darkness. Scott's naked body rose up out of the metal shell. Tubes from the cocoon were connected to his body. He regurgitated one from his mouth before struggling to remove the two below his waist. Wiping tears from his eyes Scott stepped out into the unknown terrain. The ground below his feet was soft and wet. It was dark preventing him from making out any of the landscape. The sky above him had swirling dark clouds. The air was thin as Scott took his first breaths on his own. His feet splashed through the mud as he set out walking. Scott walked for as long as he could before collapsing. Once he regained his strength he returned to his trek. Unsure of where he was or where he was heading Scott continued to walk blindly through the dark. He lost track of how long it had been before finally collapsing from hunger and dehydration. In the darkness Scott heard a faint noise as footsteps approached. The feet splashed in the mud as Scott opened his eyes to see a furry creature heading towards him. Scott quickly climbed to his feet as the monster before him let out a loud roar. A few yards away from Scott stood a grizzly bear. The bear's eyes stayed on Scott as it walked about. Scott stood still and began to shout at the predator. It looked like the bear was sizing Scott up as he continued shouting at it. The naked man attempted to stare the bear down. His eyes would glance away to survey his surroundings for an exit every few seconds. Backing away slowly Scott screamed at the bear as it began to approach. Scott knew he could not possibly outrun the grizzly as it charged at him. He had no other choice, being naked and unarmed. His naked body turned around to retreat as an arrow flew over his head. There was a cry from the bear as the arrowhead pierced it's coat. The wooden arrow protruded from the bear's shoulder as it continued its charge for Scott. A second arrow whizzed through the air. The bear slowed as two arrows now stuck out of its body. Scott kept running as he heard shouts coming from nearby rocks. Two arrows fired back to back at the bear. One missed as the other arrow landed in the bear's neck. The thick animal fell to the mud as its coat was soaked in warm blood. Scott looked back to see the bear was down as he slowed to a stop. His chest hurt as he gasped for air. It was weird not having a nose anymore. Thanks to the modifications the aliens had made Scott was quickly able to catch his breath. Hooded figures emerged from the rocks where the shouting had taken place. There were two of them in the dark as they approached Scott and the bear. One knelt down by the bear as he shouted, "This'll get us some respect at camp for sure!" The other one had made his way to Scott who was still hunched over. "You okay, buddy?" The cloaked figure asked. Scott stood up and looked at the person. Seeing Scott's face caused the figure to draw his bow. "Don't move," he cried out. Scott raised his hands above his head. The second figure came over with a small blade from his belt. "Kill this thing," the bladed man declared, "go on and shoot it." Scott shook his head at the two men and shouted, "Don't shoot, my name is Scott Carter, I'm human!" The man with the bow lowered his weapon. "What are you doing?" the man with the blade cried out. "I'm human," Scott yelled again. Thunder echoed in the distance. The man handed his bow to his ally before removing his cloak. He went to Scott and wrapped it around him. The cloak was warm around Scott's naked body. "What the hell is going on, Cj?" ordered the man now holding the bow. Scott recognized the name, but the man before him was too old to be Craig Callahan's son. Scott had just seen him a few short days ago. "If this guy's telling the truth," Cj shouted, "Then I knew him a long time ago, when all this shit first went down."

Chapter Eighteen

SCOTT CARTER WORKED WITH CJ CALLAHAN AND HIS ACCOMPLICE to drag the bear's body through the mud. "Were you guys hunting this thing?" Scott asked. Cj nodded, "it's rare that we see any animals these days," the young man informed Scott. "We knew we were hunting something big but we had no idea what," Cj spoke as his friend scoffed. "Don't worry about him," Cj remarked. Scott looked at the other guy then back to Cj. "Last I saw, you were a kid sitting in your dad's lap," Scott chuckled. Cj smiled back in the dark and countered, "You were pissing my dad off with your joint." Scott's smile turned to a frown as he thought about how badly he wanted a joint now. The three of them continued for a bit in silence before Scott broke the silence. "So where are we heading?" Scott's voice echoed signs of fatigue. Cj looked to his friend who remained silent, "We're a part of a larger expedition," the young Callahan stated. Scott tightened his grip on the rope in his hands pulling the bear. "We have a small boat not far from here, then we're heading back home," Cj smiled again as he talked. Scott thought about Daphne, "Hey Cj," He asked, "Do you remember Daphne?" Cj nodded, "Yeah, she-" Cj started to explain but he was cut off. "Our boat is just up ahead," the friend interrupted, "Save the chat for when we're on-board."

Scott helped the two men carry the bear's carcass onto the deck. Their shipmates gathered around to see the animal they'd brought. Everyone was abuzz with curiosity towards Scott. One man came through the crowd as rain started to fall on them. "Out of the way, let me get a look at it," He shouted from under his hood. The figure was taller than Scott. He pulled back his hood to reveal long dark hair. A few strands hung loosely in his face as the rest was pulled back into a bun on top of his head. His eyes looked familiar to Scott. "Javier?" Scott asked. The dark haired man lunged toward Scott and gripped him by the collar of his cloak. "Don't speak my brother's name, creature!" The man shouted. Scott was still in the man's grip as he tried to get a better look at the man. "That's Scott," Cj Callahan shouted, "Al, that's Scott Carter!" The rain was falling hard as everyone made their way below deck.

Al Rodrigues poured two drinks as Scott entered his room to join him. Scott had changed into dry clothes, although they did not smell fresh. "Jesus, Al," Scott sighed, "You look just like him," Scott remarked as Al passed him a glass. Al tossed his drink back as Scott sipped it. His body had not had water in a long time. "Where have you been?" Al questioned. Scott told him what he remembered about the alien ship, and waking up in the cocoon earlier. "So they just dropped you off, huh?" Al scoffed as his arms crossed. Scott could tell that the young man was skeptical. "Yes, honestly I have no clue why I woke up here," Scott insisted. "I figured I'd die on their ship," Scott said before taking a drink. Al raised an eyebrow, asking, "Then why do you look like those things?" Scott finished his water and then let out a sigh of relief. He looked back to Al who was waiting for an answer. "Those aliens did this to me, I didn't ask for this," Scott said softly. Al leaned forward with his eyebrow still raised. "So you disappear for ten years. Not to mention, you're the only person to ever come back, and I'm supposed to believe that you don't know how that happened?" Al questioned. Scott couldn't believe it. Had he really been on the ship that long? It was obvious given how old Cj and Al had become, but still it was difficult to comprehend. "Al, I honestly don't know. You'd have better luck asking me if I thought the sun would shine tomorrow," Scott said in a serious tone. Al finished his water then stood up. "You can sleep in the barracks with the other men, We won't be home until morning," Al said as he made his way to the door. Scott nodded and followed Al out.

The next morning Scott was woken up by the sounds of shouting and cheering. He was alone in the barracks. The noise was coming from above on the deck. He made his way out and up the stairs to join the crowd of men up top. It was bright as Scott reached the top of the stairs. Shielding his eyes Scott stepped out into the morning sun. The reflection was bright on the surface of the water. Everyone was shouting and hugging. One person screamed, "I can't believe it, the sun is back!" Scott looked around and noticed Al Rodrigues staring directly at him.

Chapter Nineteen

AL RODRIGUES LOADED HIS BAGS QUIETLY IN HIS BUNK. HIS MIND was on home and seeing his family again. Al was happy to see the sun that morning for the first time in a decade. The world had become a cold and unfamiliar place in the years following the aliens' arrival.

His bags were prepped as Al undressed and pulled a metallic suit from his gear. The suit was small, as if it could dress a child. Al's long legs slid comfortably into the expansive material. The metal was thin, and the one piece suit fit snug to his adult body. Al collected his black cloak and draped it over his back. He fastened a belt at his waist securing his sword and scabbard close. Al threw his bags over his shoulder and made his way out onto the deck. The sun was beaming down on their boat in the harbor. Scott stood at the bow of the small ship admiring the view. As Al walked up Scott turned back to him smiling. Scott's face was still a sight for Al to wrap his head around. "What city is this?" Scott questioned. Al stepped up beside him and replied, "It doesn't matter to us anymore." Scott looked at the shoreline, where a border had been made. A twenty foot wooden wall stretched out into the foggy outskirts. "We found our way here, a few months into it all," Al confessed. "We didn't know where we were going. Everyday we woke up somewhere new, and every night we looked for shelter," Al sighed.

Scott glanced back to Al. "Eventually we found this place. For whatever reason the aliens had left it untouched. Well mostly," Al spoke as he turned back to face the ship, and his crew. "We're different people Scott," Al remarked. Scott did not take his eyes off of Al Rodrigues.

Al Rodrigues escorted Scott Carter off of the boat while crewmen shouted around them. They were unloading gear and supplies as quickly as they could. They were desperate to return to their loved ones. Scott had no belongings to carry and offered to assist Al. The cloaked man refused as they left the harbor. "Scott," Al said in a firm voice, "Put your hood up the rest of the way." Scott nodded as he pulled the hood over his bald head. He did not want to cause a scene with his grey appearance. The two hooded men moved quietly together up a muddy path. The first and second floors of office buildings stood around them. The streets still had abandoned cars, left to gather rust over the years. Soon the streets were busy with pedestrians as Al led Scott further into town. The two men walked up the stairs to a large building at the end of the street. Two armed guards were at the door, carrying swords and wearing metallic suits like Al. "Are they wearing alien suits?" Scott questioned. Al glanced over to Scott as he opened the door, "We all wear them, thanks to Daphne," He replied.

Chapter Twenty

Scott Carter was surprised to see the age on some familiar faces. Al Rodrigues stepped forward removing his hood to his audience. "Councilor's, I've got someone here you'll want to meet," Al cried out. "Son, what are you doing charging in here like this?" Countered the weathered voice of Tiago Rodrigues. Scott was happy to see the white haired man. Al had told him about the night they witnessed Javier's brutal death. "Dad, listen," Al stepped forward as he spoke, "This man here with me," Al said as he turned back to the cloaked Scott. Pulling back the hood Scott revealed his altered appearance to the room. "My name is Scott Carter," He shouted. Tiago sighed as some of the other members of the council questioned the name. Another man stood up and walked around the table towards Scott. He had grown a long beard in the years since, but Scott recognized the man approaching. "Hello Craig," Scott said in a friendly voice. Craig Callahan stopped in his tracks and looked back to the other members of the council. Tiago nodded and stood. He used a cane as he moved towards Scott and his son. Al put his hand on his tired fathers shoulder. "It's good to see you back, my boy," Tiago praised his youngest son. Al turned back to Scott and asked, "Can we call for Daphne?"

The sun would be setting soon as Daphne Williams worked with a smile. She was setting up candles for the eventual nightfall. Today was a special day and she wanted to make it as perfect as possible. Sarah Callahan worked hard alongside Daphne. The two of them had developed a unique bond over the years. "You think he's going to like it?" Sarah asked. She held up a card as a banner hung overhead. The banner read, "Welcome Home." Daphne smiled at the card in the young girl's hand. "We'd better hurry up, before he gets here," Daphne remarked. The two continued working until a knock came at the door.

Scott Carter introduced himself to the rest of the council. The three remaining members looked weary of him, but took turns introducing themselves. "My name is James Landry, I lead our troops," The one armed man declared. His cloak was layered with the fur of an animal and a thin sword rested at his side.

"My name is Dana," the second council member spoke. She resembled her father greatly, and Scott recognized her before she could continue. "I believe you once worked for my father, Donald Webb," she said softly. Scott asked, "Is he here?" Dana's eyes grew glossy as she let out a sigh. "No," Dana declared, "My father gave his life that night for my own. I've been living for the both of us ever since." Scott felt her pain from across the table. The last member smiled as she introduced herself. She had shoulder length dark hair and a scar across her forehead. "I'm the newest member of the council, Karla Green," She said through her gaze. She had not taken her eyes off of Scott since he removed his hood. Scott smiled back at her as the doors behind him came crashing open. In walked Ben Miller, dressed in metal armor with two guards at his back. All three men carried swords. A young boy followed behind them. the child looked scared as he saw Scott. Ben turned back to the guards and the child. "Take Jason into the halls," Ben ordered. Turning back he stared at the alien figure in the room. "Ah, Scott, it's true," Ben exclaimed, "I see you have met my council."

Chapter Twenty-One

CJ CALLAHAN HAD WAITED PATIENTLY FOR HIS BIG DAY. TODAY HE would turn Eighteen and be allowed to join the ranks of the community's guard. To commence the festivities Craig had arranged for Al to take his only son on a hunting expedition. Cj Callahan's birthday became overshadowed by the return of Scott Carter.

Cj Callahan stood outside and marveled at the colors of the sunset. His eyes filled with tears at the beautiful sight. *Of all the days,* he thought. Cj wiped his tears and proceeded to walk home. The boat was finally unloaded and he was looking forward to seeing his dad and sister. As he approached their residence Cj noticed just how dark it was inside. *They must be surprising me,* he thought as he slowly opened the front door. Inside he was greeted to an empty house. The young man smiled to himself as he read the banner Sarah had prepared for him. On the table Cj found the hand drawn birthday card from his teen sister.

Daphne Williams and Sarah Callahan made their way into the council hall. Ben Miller was seated at the council table with everyone around him. Scott Carter and Al Rodrigues sat opposite of them with their backs to the door. As Daphne entered Scott's alien face turned around to meet her. She stopped in her tracks as she made eye contact with the deformed Scott. "So it's true?" She said with a sigh as Scott stood to greet her. "Hello beautiful," Scott said as he noticed the age on her face. Ben stood and walked around the table towards them. "What a reunion, am i right?" Ben remarked. Scott shot a glance to Ben and then back to Daphne. "Scott," Daphne cried, "It's been a long time." Scott nodded and tried to put his arms around Daphne for a hug. She pulled away from him as Ben scoffed. "This is going to be a lot for you to hear Scott," Ben said as he laughed. Ben walked over to Daphne and placed his arm around her. Scott looked at the two of them in confusion. "Scott, it's been a long time," Daphne began to say. Scott couldn't believe it. Ben's arm lingered around Daphne's shoulder as the two of them stood close. "When you-" Daphne's voice trembled. An explosion of gunfire outside the building interrupted. The doors to the room flew open as Ben's guards stepped in with swords drawn. Landry and Al were on their feet with their blades ready. The small child that was with Ben earlier ran in from the hall crying out, "Mom!" as he jumped into Daphne's arms. Scott was shocked as Daphne ran her fingers through the boy's hair embracing him. "Report!" Landry called out to the guards at the door. The two men ran to protect Daphne and her son as Ben drew his weapon from his waist. "There appears to be an alien ship above us, sir," cried one of the guards.

Gunfire erupted in the street as grey skinned aliens rampaged through the human town. The aliens were the ones firing the pistols and rifles, aiming at the buildings as they advanced. Cj Callahan emerged from the shadows undetected as two aliens ran by. Before they could turn back his cold blade cut them down. The two grey bodies fell to his feet as the young man scoffed to himself. *Some birthday,* he thought, cleaning the tar like blood from his sword.

Chapter Twenty-Two

AL RODRIGUES RAN THROUGH THE STREETS AS ALIENS WHISTLED around him. Their ship was just above the town as nightfall blanketed the sky. Al's sword was sharp. He had his brother David to thank for that. Years before all of this started, David was the kid obsessed with drawing knives and swords. Over time the aliens began carrying guns to fight back. Ammo became scarce causing the survivors to realize the value in Devmetal. The alien ships were emitting enough resources to forge the tools needed to survive. David spent years now creating swords and arrowheads for the guards. Al always commented about how he hated carrying Devmetal and wearing the suits knowing what it did to Javier. Even though the suits proved to be invaluable when the Devmetal rain fell. The suits can withstand a lot of stress, but Devmetal can be forged to cut through itself like butter.

David's weapons allowed the humans to have a chance of fighting fire with fire.

Al Rodrigues' sword had seen its share of Grey bodies. Tonight as the aliens threatened his hometown he vowed to double those numbers. As Al lunged his blade into the side of a Grey the young man fell to his knees. The shot was loud, but Al didn't seem to process it until it was over. Al drove his sword deeper into his shooter on the ground. His right hand held his shoulder tight as he applied pressure. The Devmetal suits could withstand a bullet, but it wasn't a guaranteed defense. This was the case tonight as Al collected himself in the street. He cursed to himself for getting taken out of the fight as he felt warm blood in his left sleeve.

Scott Carter rode out the mayhem from the safety of the council hall. Ben Miller and his guards stood watch after Landry and Al had gone to battle. Scott wanted to talk to Daphne more but the timing was off as she held her son across the room. Sarah and Craig Callahan embraced each other as the battle outside quieted.

The aliens had stopped pouring out of the ship above as Landry and his men secured the town. Scott and the others emerged from their building once Landry gave the all clear. Cj Callahan made his way through the crowd and up to his dad and sister. The three of them embraced, talking over each other about what happened. Sarah didn't say much during the exchange. A few Grey's had been captured and pulled to the center of the crowd. They were forced to their knees as Ben Miller approached them. Landry stood close by with his one handed sword ready. "Look what we have here," Ben yelled. The crowd cheered as the alien ship above stood by. The alien prisoners were silent as one looked over to see Scott in the crowd. The alien began to whistle as the others caught on and joined in. Ben drew his sword and cut off the head of the lead whistler. The other two aliens fell silent as the lifeless body dropped. The ship above hummed with life, like a living cloud in the night sky. The long legs of the ship began to pour down to the ground below, dozens of legs throughout the survivors town. At the base of each leg emerged dozens of Grey's. Landry and his men charged the aliens in the night as panic broke out in the ruined streets. Ben was ready to engage in the action when one of the prisoners cried out. It pointed at Scott and in a deep voice declared, "An infiltrator walks among them." Scott was confused by the accusation as Ben executed the two remaining prisoners.

The aliens had numbers on their side but the brute strength of the humans drove them off. As the cold metal legs of the ship began to retract aliens scrambled to make it back to their kind. Craig Callahan had been huddled with his daughter tight in his arms during the raid. The teen girl began to push and scream once the ship departed. She bit her father's wrist causing him to back off in pain as she lunged to her feet. "Sarah!" Craig called after the teen as she ran. Cj Callahan looked up from the kill at his feet to see his sister join the aliens fleeing toward their ship. Stragglers were killed unmercifully as the menacing ship faded into the distance.

Chapter Twenty-Three

CASUALTIES FROM BOTH SIDES WERE COLLECTED TO BE BURNED IN the night. The dead corpses of the Grey's provided Devmetal suits and weapons for the people to claim. As this happened Scott Carter was placed under arrest by Ben Miller. Daphne tried to step in but her son Jason was crying and uncooperative as Ben led Scott away. Landry gave a few words for the fallen while bright flames danced around him. Craig and Cj Callahan turned their backs on what was happening to Scott. They assisted with the clean up arrangements without speaking to one another. It was clear though, that both of the Callahan men had Sarah on their minds.

"Please, Ben," Scott pleaded as he walked through the town. The same armed guards that had protected Scott earlier now escorted him with swords at his back. "What are the odds," Ben fired back, "You show up after ten years and not even ten hours go by before the aliens attack. Not to mention you look just like those- freaks," Ben's remarks sat with Scott for a second. He didn't have a reply. "What did the Grey's do to you?" Ben continued.

Al Rodrigues' apartment was silent as his older brother David worked by candlelight. Al's shoulder was on fire even after his brother finished cleaning his wound. David had become good with his hands over the years. He had become a capable blacksmith but also Al's personal nurse. The years since the Grey's arrival forced the boys to mature. Both men had outlived their brother Javier and learned to make peace with his death.

David sat back and wiped the sweat from his brow. The front door gently opened in the other room before footsteps approached. Tiago Rodrigues removed his cap and placed it on the table beside his sons. Before anyone could speak the two young men stood and hugged their father. "You are good boys for taking care of each other," Tiago said in a soft humbled tone. Their embrace ended as Tiago moved faster than they had seen him move in years as he made his way toward Al's bedroom. "Pa," David shouted, "Where's the rush?" David looked back to Al who was once again seated at the table. Al examined his bandaged shoulder. A moment later Tiago emerged with a small object in his hand. Al glanced up to his father and saw the device in his possession. "Wait, no!" Al barked as he lunged to his feet. Tiago held up the instant camera in his hand. It had once been in the possession of Al's brother Javier. Tiago insisted on using the camera whenever he got the chance, despite his son's vocal protest. "This is the last time I'll use it, son. It was in Javier's bag for a reason," Tiago explained. Al scoffed at his father. David had taken Al's vacant seat at the table. "Dad," David began, "assuming it still works, what are you taking a picture of?" The elder brother asked while his father went to the door.

Scott Carter felt a breeze on his neck as Ben led him down a lonely street. The two approached a building at the end of the block. There were guards at the entrance of the small building. The two story structure had no windows on the lower level. The windows on the upper floor of the brick building had bars covering the glass. It appeared to be heavily guarded and fortified. Ben escorted Scott inside past the guards. The interior was quiet as Scott followed Ben up the stairs. As they walked through the candlelit hall Ben looked back over his shoulder. "I'm surprised you've been this silent," Ben remarked. Scott stared up from the floor toward his former manager. "What happened to you?" Scott questioned. Ben kept his focus on the hall in front of them as they made their way to the end. Ben pushed open the door as Scott lingered behind him. Ben motioned for Scott to step inside. "Ben, is this necessary?" Scott pleaded. Ben remained silent. Behind them a noise came from the stairs. *It must be Daphne,* Scott thought. The grey skinned human turned back to see Tiago and his two sons. "Al, are you okay?" Ben called out, seeing the young man's bandage. Scott remained the focus of Ben's attention as the three men joined them. "It won't slow me down," Al replied. Scott looked to the family for support. "Are you guys here to help?" Scott asked. Al shook his head. "Ben, I was wondering if I may take his picture," Tiago stated with the camera in hand. Scott was surprised that Tiago did not ask him directly. Ben smirked and looked over to Tiago. "Okay, but make it quick," Ben laughed. Scott stood awkwardly before the group as Tiago flashed his camera. A few seconds later the film slowly rolled out. "Okay, let's get back to it," Ben demanded. Scott was embarrassed from the experience and offered no resistance. He walked into the room with Ben on his heels. The interior was larger than Scott was expecting. There were offices that had been barred off into makeshift prison cells. It was dark and quiet as Scott stepped into his cell. Ben shut the barred gate behind him and locked it. Tiago and his sons had left the hall outside. Ben and Scott were alone in the prison. As Ben turned around to leave Scott cried out again. "What the hell happened to you?" Scott cried. Ben shut the door behind him without looking back. Scott was alone in his spacious cell. He assumed it was the first time the cell had been needed. The floor was cold as Scott sat down. There wasn't much else to do in there. Across the room from his cell there was a grumble. Scott leaned forward on one knee. "Someone there?" a voice called out. The words were dry as they echoed through the dark. Scott stood up, "I was wondering the same thing," he said. Scott stepped towards the bars at the front of his cell. "You got a name?" Scott asked. From the darkness the voice answered, " I do. Jacob." A silhouette appeared in the dark. The figure's white hair was visible as it reached the front of the cell. "Most people just call me Mr. Bolton," the old man said with a smile. Scott laughed in his lonely cell. "I could say the same," Mr. Bolton commented on Scott's laughter. "You look ridiculous son," The old man quipped. Scott placed his forehead against the bars of his cell. "I'm surprised you recognized me so quickly," Scott remarked. Mr. Bolton ran his fingers through his own white hair and beard. He looked like a different man than when Scott had last seen him. "When you get to be my age it's not about looks anymore," Mr. Bolton told Scott. "Those aliens can paint you up and down but I still heard Scott Carter screaming at Ben when you got here. That's how I knew," Mr. Bolton replied before sitting on the cot in his cell. Hearing those words made Scott momentarily happy. "I-, we, thought you died that night," Mr. Bolton confessed. "Hell, I saw Tom ripped clean in half by those Grey's. They pulled on him until he split, bone's and all," Bolton sighed, and he signed the cross for his friend. Scott got a chill up his spine. "We survived for as long as we could, after a while we knew we couldn't make it with our manpower," Mr. Bolton continued. "We had maybe thirty survivors after that Country Club. So we knew we had to get somewhere. Daphne had lost you, or at least thought she had. Ben's wife Kelly really stepped up to be there for her in your absence," Mr. Bolton said as he glanced at Scott. The young man's attention was focused on Mr. Bolton's recount. "Where is she?" Scott asked, not only was he asking about Kelly Miller, but where was Daphne? Scott hoped any minute Daphne would burst in and get him out. "She's here, Daphne's safe last I heard," Mr. Bolton assured Scott of what he already knew. "No, I know that, but where's Kelly now?" Scott Carter asked, unsure why he had such a sudden interest in Ben's wife. Mr. Bolton straightened up his old back on the small cot he had spent every night on, praying for comfort. "Well, that's the tough part," Bolton sighed. "I got her killed not long after settling us here," the old man's voice broke a little. Scott slumped back on the floor. Mr. Bolton did not say anything else and Scott did not ask. Scott understood what he needed to know about Ben Miller. As Scott drifted to sleep on the floor of his cell his mind stayed on Kelly Miller. When Scott dreamed that night he saw her, and she was grey in his image. Sarah Callahan accompanied Kelly in grey form, before another familiar face greeted Scott.

Chapter Twenty-Four

SCOTT DREAMED ABOUT BIRDS CHIRPING IN THE TREES AS HE explored the woods below. His brown fur swayed in the wind as he sniffed after his prey. Ahead of Scott there was an unsuspecting deer passing through the trees. Scott ran on four legs after the carcass of the deer in front of him. The flesh of the deer had rotted away exposing muscle and bone underneath. Scott caught the young buck as his claws sunk into its coat. His jaw was tight around the neck of his prey. There were flies gathering around the body as Scott consumed every last piece. When he finished he stood back on his hind legs and roared.

Cj Callahan woke Scott up from his dream. In the months since Scott's incarceration Cj had volunteered to join the prison guard. "Scott, you were right," Cj shouted from the doorway. The young man wore his Devmetal suit as usual, with a hooded bear skin cloak over it. The brown fur of the bear reminded Scott of two things. The day Cj saved his life, and his dream as a bear just now. Cj pulled back his hood, which was made from the bear's head. The nose of the animal hide rested on his forehead like the bill of a hat. Scott sat up as Cj waved in his direction. "Are you guys back from your hunt?" Scott asked. Scott rubbed his eyes as Cj approached his cell. Scott rose up from the floor where he slept and joined Cj at the door. Despite being hairless Scott had managed to grow some stubble on his face. Scott scratched his chin as Cj looked over to Mr. Bolton's cell. The white haired man sat on the floor of his cell, paying no attention to the others . Cj looked back to the grey Scott opposite of him, behind bars. "We got back last night," Cj said, answering Scott's question about the hunt. Cj's smile grew as he continued, declaring "You were right." Scott was confused, so he asked, "Right about what?" Cj laughed then looked over to Mr. Bolton's cell. "Hey, Mr. B," Cj shouted. Mr. Bolton perked up on the floor and turned around to face them. The young guard walked toward Mr. Bolton's cell and leaned against the door frame. "You remember what Scott said about spring?" Cj wondered. Mr. Bolton shrugged. "The days run together in here," Scott called out from his cell. "You'll have to be specific," Mr. Bolton replied. Cj smiled and grabbed his bear skin cloak. "It was right before the winter came. I wore this fur for the first time and Scott said I was going to need it." Cj began. Scott looked to the window in the room. The angle of his cell prevented him from seeing more than the daylight shining in. "Was that what I was right about?" Scott asked. Cj shook his head, "Not that part. Later that day you talked about growing trees and grass in the spring." Scott began to laugh. Cj walked back to Scott's cell. "What's so funny?" Cj asked. "Nothing," Scott replied. Cj looked back at Mr. Bolton who was just as confused. "Anyway," Cj said, "While we were out we ran into green grass and even a tree with sprouts growing on the branches." Cj glanced back and forth between the men. "That's incredible right?" Cj remarked. Mr. Bolton smiled wide. Cj looked back to Scott and asked, "So how did you know?" Scott laughed and scratched at his itchy stubble. "Honestly," Scott explained, "I was joking about growing my own weed."

Al Rodrigues sat at the council table as they talked amongst themselves. With the seasons changing Landry and the council had ordered more expeditions. Food and resources were running low thanks to the winter months. "One more thing," Al declared over the chatter. Tiago and the others fell silent. "What is it?" Karla Green asked. Al looked to the five of them across the table. "Well it's Cj Callahan," Al said as he looked over to Craig. "What about him?" Dana Webb inquired. "Cj thinks that Scott Carter had something to do with his team's discovery," Al informed them. "What do you think?" Tiago asked his son. "I think," Al started, "I think it's bad for our men to be influenced by that kind of talk. It's bad for people in the locker room to get word on." Al glanced at each council member. Craig leaned back in his seat. Landry sat back comfortably in his chair processing Al's report. "Perhaps my son has been spending too much time at the prison," Craig suggested. "Perhaps," Dana remarked, "But his friendship with the alien could be useful." Al nodded. He had not seen Scott in person since the night of the attack. "How about we ground him, keep him away from the others for a bit and put him on prison duty full time?" Tiago questioned. "I think that could be good," Al said. Tiago nodded to Dana and Karla. "Okay," Tiago stated. Landry leaned forward in his seat as he spoke, "Cj will sit out any runs for the unforeseeable future." Craig Callahan scoffed at this idea. "Unfortunately, I would like you to take your men back out after twenty four hours of rest," Landry continued. Al's eyes widened as he glanced towards his father. Al had just returned home from hunting that morning. "He's right son, we're counting on you.

Take a boat and head south," Tiago instructed his son. Craig was silent, angry that the council had given up any searches for Sarah.

Cj Callahan went upstairs to check on the two prisoners before his shift ended. The sun was setting outside as he lit a few candles for the two men. "Scott, you okay?" Cj called out once he saw him. There was vomit pooled around his body on the floor. "He threw up and collapsed," Mr. Bolton stated. Cj stepped up to the bars of Scott's cell for a closer look. "Scott?" Cj called out again. There was movement on the floor as Scott sat up. "I'm okay," Scott replied, "I just can't stop thinking about this dream I had last night." Cj watched Scott wipe his mouth with the sleeve of his worn out shirt. "In my dream I was eating a dead animal," Scott commented, "Kind of makes you think twice about what you put into your body."

Chapter Twenty-Five

IN THE YEARS SINCE THE GREY'S ARRIVAL A COFFEE MUG SURVIVED only to find its way into Ben Miller's possession. Ben finished his morning coffee on his upper balcony. He lived in a two story town-home a few blocks away from the council hall. The streets below were busy as crowds of people rushed to start their day. Someone shouted from the street below as Ben tossed back the last of his drink. He stood up and looked down over the rail to see two of his councilors. Craig Callahan stepped into Ben's home along with Dana Webb as he motioned for them to sit. Dana shook her head to decline as she greeted him. "We're not going to be staying long," Craig informed his leader. Ben took his mug to the kitchen as he called out over his shoulder. "That's perfect," Ben shouted. Dana looked over to her elder council member. "Tell him," Dana whispered under her breath. Ben returned to his two guests empty handed. "So, what brings you two by this early?" Ben asked. Craig made eye contact with Dana before looking back to Ben. "Well," Craig started, "Maybe I will sit down." He took a seat on Ben's couch as Dana rolled her eyes. The furniture in Ben's home was worn out, but the fabric was still intact. Craig relaxed into the cushioned seat. His old back felt relief as Ben stood over him. "It's about the alien, Scott," Dana started. Ben turned back to look at the woman still in his doorway. "What about him?" Ben questioned. Craig leaned forward, feeling the tension in his lower back. "No, no, no," Craig said, shaking his head. "It's my son," he confessed. Dana came closer to the two men as she stopped a few feet from Ben. "Well, what about him this time?" Ben demanded. Craig cleared his throat. "First of all, I want to say how grateful I am to see my son become the man he is today," Craig began. "After losing my Sarah last fall," Craig said with a tear. "Well hell, everyone in this room is familiar with loss at this point," he cried. Ben looked down as he clenched his fist. Craig continued, "Now Ben, we're all happy to do the mandatory lock-in during winter. Really, our workers thrive on keeping our essentials going. But after being locked in their homes for months these people out there need activity." Ben looked confused, "So what would you suggest?" He asked. Dana scoffed and stepped forward. "Nothing!" she fired off, "Dammit Craig, quit beatin' around the bush. Tell him or I will." Dana took a deep breath after her outburst. Craig remained silent. Ben was still on his feet and grew annoyed with the pair. "Out with it!" Ben shouted. Dana adjusted a loose strand of hair out of her face. She replied, "Craig's son loves that alien guy. The poor kid can't stop talking about him," Dana laughed as the last of her words left her lips. "That's a damn lie," Craig rebuffed. Dana laughed again. "Well you were taking your time," She chuckled. Ben placed his hand on Craig's shoulder. "Tell me what you came to say," Ben demanded in a calm voice. "My son won't shut up about Scott Carter," Craig confessed. "We put him on prison duty a few weeks ago to keep him away from the other men. But it was too late. Cabin fever and rumors about the alien in our prison were too much to contain," Craig said. Ben coughed, then asked, "What are you telling me?" Craig scratched an itch on his nose.

"People are getting out of their homes, to see the alien," Craig sighed, "And my son is letting it happen."

Ben Miller marched through the crowded streets with Dana and Craig at his back. His sword was ready on his waist as pedestrians stepped out of his path. The prison was just ahead of the three as the crowd around them broke out in cheers. The gallops of horses could be heard in the distance. Ben looked around with his right hand ready on his weapon. The people flooded the street as Al Rodrigues and his men were revealed as the source of the commotion. The young man was mounted atop a black horse. Two other soldiers behind him rode horses of equal size and beauty. "Scott and your son will have to wait," Ben declared to his councilors. The leader of the community made his way over to his people as the crowd rejoiced.

Chapter Twenty-Six

AL RODRIGUES REUNITED WITH HIS FATHER TIAGO AND THE council. His mission had been successful. "We went about as far as we could," Al informed the group. Ben Miller sat at the head of the table while everyone listened. "I'll admit we were ready to come home empty handed, until we saw them," Al revealed. Karla Green spoke up from her council seat. "The Grey's?" She questioned. "No," Al insisted. Ben glanced over to the woman. "Please, let him speak," Ben commanded. Al did not waste a breath before he continued. "Birds," The young Rodrigues man spoke. "Hundreds of birds clouded the skies above us. I thought it was the Devmetal raining down at first. Either way they were countered by the firepower of my troops." The council's faces lit up as they processed the news. "Did you bring enough to eat?" Ben asked. Al nodded. "There's more," Al revealed. "After the birds, we saw more wildlife return. We brought back plenty to feed the entire community," Al smiled as he said the words. "What about those horses?" Tiago inquired. Al still had a smile on his face as he looked over to his father. "We rescued those horses from the Grey's" Al remarked. "Did you find Sarah?" Craig Callahan blurted out. Al shook his head. "No, I'm sorry," the young man's words echoed in Craig's ears. "When we found where the aliens were keeping their horses we freed them. Then myself and a few men waited behind for the grey's to return. Bastards thought they were coming to get their horses but they got us instead," Al bragged. Landry smiled and gave the young man a nod.

As the council finished up their questions Cj Callahan stormed into the room. He had his bear pelt on but no weapon. "Cj, we did not request you join us," Landry called out to the guest. "Son, what is this about?" Craig demanded. Cj made eye contact with Al at the table. "Al, is it true you guys had a successful hunt?" Cj questioned. Al nodded. "Cj, what's the meaning of this?" Craig asked his son. Ben stood up and walked around the table. "No, let's hear what the young man has to say," Ben stated as he walked. Making his way around the table Ben was now standing beside Cj. "Continue," Ben said calmly. Cj spoke directly to Ben. "Scott has been predicting a lot of things," the young guard pointed out. "Al, don't forget what you saw that first day we found him," he said, turning to his captain at the table. Al thought about his conversation with Scott and the sunshine the following morning. "Doesn't change what he is," Dana Webb popped off from the table. Ben smiled. Cj shrugged and continued his case, "Scott knows something we don't. A few weeks ago he warned me about this hunt Al." Curiosity had swelled up inside Al Rodrigues as he heard Cj. Before Al could speak Cj warned everyone. "Scott doesn't want us to eat the meat," Cj cried. Ben scoffed as the council behind him seemed to do the same. "He would rather have us starve?" Ben laughed. "And to think I wanted us to celebrate tonight, I guess that's off the table," Ben said with a smirk. Dana Webb leapt from her chair. "Our people could use a night of celebration after the winter we've had!" Dana exclaimed. Karla

Green nodded as she spoke, "She's right Ben, it would be good for worker morale." Ben looked back to his councilors with a scowl. "I'll let you two plan the evening festivities then," Ben insisted. He turned his attention back to Cj Callahan who was still in front of him. "As for you," Ben said in a serious tone. "I hear that Scott has been getting visitors. Either you stop allowing that to happen or we'll fill another cell. You understand me?" Ben scolded. "I don't care if you are on the council Craig," Ben raised his voice to address Craig behind him. Cj felt a chill go up his spine.

Chapter Twenty-Seven

BEN MILLER ESCORTED CJ CALLAHAN BACK TO WORK AT THE prison. The man left his group of five councilors to plan a festival for that evening after sunset. Cj was quiet after being scolded in front of his father and superiors. The two of them made it to the two story prison where Scott Carter was held. A small group of people were outside the locked doors. They rose up off the ground after seeing Cj return. Ben grew angry realizing how comfortable the people had become with visitation. Cj Callahan unlocked the doors for Ben who entered the prison. "They better be gone when I come back," Ben demanded. Cj nodded that he would get it done and shut the door. Ben could hear the shouts outside behind him as he reached the stairs. The door at the top of the stairs was cracked open. On the other side would be Scott and Mr. Bolton's prison cells. Ben called out Scott's name before he slowly pushed the door open.

"You just love to be in charge don't you?" Scott asked from the floor of his cell. The light was dim as the small windows provided what they could. Ben walked in and leaned against the bars of Scott's cell. "Managing people comes natural to me," Ben replied. Scott stood up from the floor and met Ben at the gate. "This isn't the car wash," Scott remarked. Ben smiled at Scott. "I'm surprised you remember," Ben said.

Scott stared at his former manager. There was a clank in the room that broke the two men's gaze. Ben looked around quickly then shouted, "keep it down old man." His eyes left Mr. Bolton's cell and returned to Scott Carter. The beard on his alien face had grown out over the weeks, restoring a shred of his former identity. "I know you did something to Cj's head," Ben warned. Scott arched his hairless brow. "I didn't do anything to that kid," Scott laughed. Ben pressed his face to the bars, "The kid thinks you dream the future," he remarked, "Like you're some kind of prophet." Scott's laughter caused tears to form in his eyes. "I don't think so," Scott said as he collected his breath. Ben leaned away from the cell. "Poor kid is convinced we should starve. Says you told him not to eat what our hunters collected," Ben laughed. Scott thought for a moment before remembering his dreams a few weeks prior. "I did dream about eating a dead deer and it made me sick," Scott confessed. Ben turned away from Scott's cell and headed for the exit. "Goodbye, Scott," Ben laughed as he slammed the door behind him.

Scott Carter sat alone in his cell until he knew Ben was gone. "You can come out," He said quietly. Out of the darkness of the room Daphne Williams emerged. She approached Scott's cell and held the bars. "I can't believe you're with that guy now," Scott scoffed. Daphne frowned. "When I lost you I was scared," Daphne cried. "Because I didn't want to do this alone," she confessed. Scott placed his hand on hers. "Ben and Kelly were there for me when I needed them. After Ben lost his wife we just found ourselves together," Daphne said through tears. Scott kept quiet as he held Daphne's hand. He wanted to bring up Daphne's son. "Scott?" Daphne asked. "Can I ask you something?" She looked up at him for an answer. "Anything," Scott said. Daphne sighed before she asked, "You do know you're Jason's father, right? Or did they change you so much you can't recognize your own son?"

Chapter Twenty-Eight

AL RODRIGUES CLEANED UP TO ACCOMPANY HIS BROTHER TO THE festival. He washed his face and combed his long hair while whistling a tune from his childhood. Al put his hair back into his usual bun before returning to his bedroom. The young man put his cold Devmetal suit on first. The one piece suit extended from his feet up to his neck. Over that Al wore a button up shirt and faded pants.

David Rodrigues sat at the kitchen table waiting for his brother to finish. He was not one for personal appearances, or festivities. His mind was in his workshop and the sword he was forging for Al. During his last expedition Al had found another source of capable Devmetal to craft. David was delighted to work with the alien metal again. He found peace in his craft, knowing the Devmetal would be used for good to counter the harm it caused him.

Ben Miller stood on the balcony of his home overlooking the crowd gathering. Tables had been arranged below and the councilors were taking their seats. The air had the aroma of cooked meats and smoke, as men and women worked tirelessly to deliver the feast. The center of the crowd consisted of the civilian population. They did not have tables or chairs. Instead they brought blankets and used cloaks to sit on. Circling the people were the guards who remained in uniform. Most of them were on duty still and took turns keeping watch.

Ben heard a noise from behind him. He looked back into his home to see Daphne Williams. Her son Jason was with her. Ben turned back to the crowd and motioned to a man below. Taking Ben's cue the man used his sword to cut the rope tied to a banner. The fabric had been hung from Ben's balcony. The crowd fell silent as they read the message it contained. "Welcome everyone," Ben shouted to his crowd.

David and Al Rodrigues walked through the crowd of guards to meet up with their father. The two of them had been invited to sit with Tiago and the council. Ben continued to shout, "I've worked hard to put this evening together for us. We had a long winter, but we got through it together. Tonight we celebrate all your hard work and perseverance." Ben had the crowd's attention. People clapped and cheered. Some of the guards were not feeling the same gratitude. "You know this thing is mandatory," one guard scoffed. Al glanced around to see if he recognized them. "Not if they want you working, like us," another guard fired back. David put his hand on his brother's shoulder urging him to continue walking. Ben's speech continued, "Our community has come a long way. Some of us have been together since the first days. Others joined our ranks as the years went by. We haven't seen a new face recently but when we do I think it's best they know who we are."

Al was ready to continue with David until one of the guards popped off. "Hey Cj, ain't it bullshit you're stuck back here while this guy gets to go up front," The guard laughed. Al turned back with anger hearing his subordinates mock him. Cj Callahan was sitting with a group of laughing guards. Al approached the four of them. Ben continued his speech behind them. "You four better watch it," Al scolded. Cj crossed his arms. "Or what?" a guard challenged. David placed his hand on Al's shoulder again. "Deal with them tomorrow, let's go eat," David pleaded. Al took a good look at Cj and his friends. He wanted to remember their faces later. Al and his brother turned to leave but Cj had something to add. "Scott says we shouldn't eat this," Cj Callahan yelled. The young man stood up with his three friends joining him. Al and David ignored them and proceeded through the crowd.

"With all that said," Ben laughed, "I realized what this place needed." He waved his hand down to the banner below. "You've probably all had the chance to read it by now. Let me be the first to say, Welcome to Paragon," Ben smiled as he recited the three words written across his banner.

After his speech Ben hugged Daphne. "We should go downstairs and join everyone," He said. Jason gave Ben a hug as Daphne watched. "We need to talk," She said after a moment of silence. Ben shook his head to agree, "Later," He replied, "Right now let's go eat."

Chapter Twenty-Nine

"WE SHOULD HAVE LISTENED TO YOU," TIAGO RODRIGUES SIGHED. His voice cracked in his old age. Scott Carter listened with curious ears. The morning sun illuminated the prison interior. Scott's bars cast a shadow over his grey face. "You warned us not to eat that foul meal," Tiago scowled. He held the collar of his cloak over his mouth as he spoke. "That's what I keep hearing," Scott remarked. His unawareness of the situation caused Tiago to tear up. The thirty-six hours since the festival had brought misery to Paragon. "Most were showing symptoms as early as yesterday morning. By the afternoon we had our first death," Tiago stated. Mr. Bolton listened from his cell. "I'm afraid for my son," Tiago pleaded. "I don't want to lose another son," he said softly. Tears ran down his wrinkled cheek.

Al Rodrigues sat close to his brother David. The elder brother was pale with a layer of sweat on his brow. Beside them was a bucket for David to vomit in. "You're a good brother, Al," David whispered between breaths. Al grabbed his brother's hand and gripped it. "You're going to fight this," Al insisted. David shook his head, "No," he whispered. "We both know you're the fighter in the family," David groaned as he spoke. Al's vision blurred as his tears formed. "Go to my workshop," David continued. "It's not quite finished but I-" David choked on his own words before he coughed up bile. Al wiped his brother's lips with a towel. "Gross," David laughed as he relaxed. Al smiled at his sick brother. "I made you something," David confessed. Al wiped the sweat from David's forehead. "Thank you," Al said, "I'll go pick it up once you feel better."

Daphne Williams had been avoiding Ben since the night of the festival. She had every intention of ending their relationship that night. The atmosphere of the festival and everyone's happiness caused her to delay the action. The next morning brought word of food poisoning and Daphne was delayed again. She told herself all morning that today would be the day. After she fed her son Jason his breakfast she prepared herself. Her Devmetal suit's reflection stood out in her bedroom mirror. The mirror had been a birthday gift from Ben the previous year. Before she put her clothes on Daphne collected a small knife to wear on her waist. Once she was completely dressed she got Jason ready. The two of them left their small apartment wearing their cloaks. She held her son's hand as he walked through the sunny streets at her side.

Tiago left Scott and Mr. Bolton alone in their cells. The two of them did not say much to each other for over an hour. Mr. Bolton broke the silence as he heard footsteps approaching. Cj Callahan entered the room wearing his bear pelt. Scott had always admired that pelt. "Cj, it's been awhile son," Mr. Bolton remarked. Scott nodded. Cj pulled back the hood of his pelt to reveal himself. There was shock on the teens face. "What is it?" Scott asked. "My dad's dead," Cj cried. Mr. Bolton lowered his head in respect to his old friend. "Did it happen like the others?" Scott questioned. Cj nodded as he wiped away tears. "Scott, what did you say to Mr. Rodrigues to get him so spooked?" Cj replied.

There was a knock at Ben Miller's front door. He was in his dining room with Daphne before the interruption. Jason played on the couch in the other room. Ben swung open his front door. The weather outside was changing as the wind had picked up. The sun was fighting to get through the clouds drifting over Paragon. "Hello Ben," James Landry stated from outside. Behind the one armed man was the rest of the council. The four of them stood close together and looked upset. "What's this about?" Ben ordered. Dana Webb spoke up from behind Landry. "Craig's dead," She said. Ben looked at his council. "Aren't you going to invite us in?" Tiago called out.

Chapter Thirty

BEN MILLER LED HIS COUNCIL INTO HIS HOME. AS THE FIVE OF them entered the room Daphne stood at the table. "I should probably leave," she laughed. Dana Webb and Karla Green made their way over to Daphne. They exchanged hugs with Daphne before finding seats at the table. "If you don't mind," Tiago suggested. Landry walked over to join his fellow councilors at the table. He had his one hand on the hilt of his sword. Daphne began to exit the room before Ben grabbed her arm. "Why don't you and Jason stick around until this is over," Ben insisted. Daphne pulled away from his grasp. "Why?" she questioned. Ben looked back over his shoulder to the council waiting on him. "Please," Ben asked, "Do this last thing for me?" Daphne could tell Ben was hurt by their sudden break up. She nodded and turned to wait with her son in the other room.

Ben took a seat at his kitchen table. There was an empty chair beside him. Tiago sat opposite from Ben. Next to Tiago was James Landry. He drew his sword and sat it on the table. Dana Webb and Karla Green each had their own end of the table. The tip of Landry's blade pointed down the table toward Karla Green.

"We need to talk about Scott," Tiago began. Ben cut him off. "Scott?" he laughed. "You're not here to talk about Craig?" Ben inquired. "We are," Dana Webb insisted. Ben leaned forward over the table. His forearms rested on the edge of the wooden surface. "Well, go on," Ben scowled. Tiago cleared his throat. "Scott warned us, but we were too busy celebrating," Tiago said in a firm voice. "I fear that my son David might be another victim of this mess," the councilor declared. Karla placed her hand on Tiago's shoulder to comfort him. Ben leaned back in his seat. Landry studied Ben as he moved about in his chair. "So what would you have me do now?" Ben scoffed at his question, before continuing, "You guys want to put Scott on the council? Looks like we've got an opening!" Ben's thumb motioned to the vacant chair beside him as he spoke. Dana Webb rolled her eyes. "Be considerate," Dana scolded, "Craig left behind a son." Ben leaned back in his seat crossing his arms. "We had not considered taking that kind of action," Tiago said. "Getting back to your question about Scott. Perhaps he should be on the council," Tiago continued. "No," Ben said as he slammed his fist into the table. "You guys get to make decisions, but if I say no then that's that," Ben relaxed as he talked. Landry took his attention off of Ben and looked to Tiago beside him. "Tell Ben what you heard this morning," Landry urged. Ben perked up with intrigue. "What is it?" Ben demanded. Tiago cleared his throat once more. "Scott told me he has been dreaming about the aliens returning," Tiago informed the group. "You didn't tell us this," Karla remarked. Tiago looked into her eyes. Before he could say anything Ben blurted out, "When?" Tiago kept his attention on Karla. "We can't be sure. I only informed Landry so that he could get the city guard alerted," Tiago declared. Landry nodded along with the words. Ben felt anger growing inside him. Knowing that the aliens returning was a possibility pissed him off. The idea of the aliens still terrified him after a decade of fending them off. Fear and their willingness to work with Scott caused Ben to become unhinged. "I don't want anyone listening to that thing," Ben shouted. "You can call it Scott but it's just another one of them to me," He continued.

"We'll have a vote," Dana Webb declared. Ben was angry hearing this. He wanted them to see things his way. "I'm in favor of releasing Scott and giving him a chance," Dana stated. Landry sat up straight in his chair. It was his turn to vote. "Well," Landry said, "I don't know much about the guy. I just want to keep everyone safe. If you don't want him on the council Ben, then that's fine, so long as we prepare for these aliens." Landry crossed his arms again after he gave his vote. Ben smiled hearing Landry's loyalty. Tiago was next to speak. "We had our differences in the beginning," he said. "Whatever happens next will impact this city greatly. You can't offer that alone Ben, none of us can. That's why we formed the council so no one man would be accountable for the community. Now we should welcome Scott into that community, and onto this council," Tiago argued. Ben stared down at his hands. He was angry with Tiago. The final vote came down to Karla Green. If she sided with Tiago and Dana then it was over for Ben. "You probably want the alien too," Ben sighed. He continued to stare at his palms. Karla shifted in her seat. It was up to her. "Well," She started, "Yes."

That was it. Ben Miller had lost. His anger grew as he clenched his fists. Tiago leaned forward in his seat to address the table. "That settles it Ben," Tiago stated. Ben thought about everyone he lost to the Grey's. The thought caused him to see red. In one motion Ben lunged to his feet. The action tossed his chair to the floor behind him. James Landry reacted, reaching for his sword on the table. Ben beat him to the weapon. In one motion Ben brought the blade down, severing the remaining hand of James Landry. Agonizing screams echoed as Landry looked at his dismembered limb. Before anyone could stand Ben jerked the wedged blade from the table. As he swung the metal its tip connected with Tiago Rodrigues' throat. Blood poured down into the collar of the elder man's shirt as he gasped for air.

Ben Miller's town home erupted with screams as Daphne Williams held her son tight. She ran through the dark streets as the house behind her fell silent.

Chapter Thirty-One

AL RODRIGUES UNLOCKED THE DOOR TO HIS BROTHER DAVID'S workshop. The interior was quiet as he shut the wooden door behind him. A lonely window by the entrance provided the light inside the small one room shop. David's desk was in the back corner. Al approached it to find a long strip of leather concealing something. He pulled back the tan skin to reveal the crafted Devmetal. David had forged a broadsword styled after a wing. The detail was incredible down to the feather. The blade was lightweight despite its size. Al swung the winged blade effortlessly through the air. *Javier would like this,* he thought. There was a leather strap on the table that Al picked up. He tried to get it around his waist before giving up and fastening it over his shoulder. The cross guard of the blade had hooks on both sides of it. Al threw the blade over his shoulder as the hook caught on the leather straps. He pulled his black cloak over his head as he exited the building.

As Al walked through the street to return home he noticed a crowd formed near Ben Miller's home. Al made his way over with his winged blade on his back. His old sword on his waist had been rendered useless. Ben was on his upper balcony shouting to the crowd. "We will get through this together everyone," Ben shouted. Al spotted a guard in the crowd and approached him. "Is he talking about the food poisoning?" Al asked. The guard nodded. His wife was beside him and she leaned in. "It got pretty bad today," She informed him. "Yeah, Ben said the whole council died from the sickness," the guard chimed in. Al's legs lost their strength as his weight pulled him to the ground. His father was healthy just this morning before going to talk with Scott. Al stood up as he heard a whistle in the crowd. He recognized the figure wearing a bear pelt motioning for him.

Cj Callahan and Al Rodrigues entered the prison together. Upstairs they were greeted by Daphne Williams and her son Jason. Al received a hug from Daphne as tears ran down her cheeks. "I'm sorry," She whispered. Al hugged Daphne a bit longer. Her embrace brought back brief memories with his own mother. The three of them approached Scott's cell while Jason stood back. "Ben's going to come for you soon," Daphne cried out. Scott stared into her worried eyes. Outside the sound of rain came to life. Al looked over to Cj and smiled. "We're going to let him," Al remarked.

Daphne held Jason's hand through the rain as they left the prison. Accompanying her were two cloaked figures with swords on their hips. The four moved swiftly together as Cj's pelt soaked with rain. Lightning flashed in the sky overhead as the roar of thunder followed. They were almost to Daphne's home as the siren's in Paragon went off. They had been commissioned after the last alien attack. Daphne looked to the sky above as rain fell in her face. The sirens were only to be used if a ship was spotted. Lightning once again made its mark on the sky. Nothing. There was no ship above them. Gunfire erupted on the outskirts of town causing Jason to cry out. Cj Callahan left the others once they reached

Daphne's front door. The combined sound of distant gunfire and screams outside grew. Daphne peaked from her front window as two grey aliens on horses rode through the street.

Chapter Thirty-Two

BEN MILLER MARCHED THROUGH THE RAINY STREETS OF PARAGON. His sword dripped with the dark blood of grey aliens. The weapon had belonged to Landry until today when Ben claimed it as his. He had two of his guards accompany him through the aliens' assault. The setting was perfect for him to kill Scott Carter. Horses stomped through the pools of rain forming in the streets. Some had riders, but most of them had been abandoned in the battle. Ahead of Ben and his guards stood a single Grey. The two guards stood back as Ben kept a calm pace forward. The alien looked up to see the man approaching. It whistled it's horrific scream as it scrambled through the rain. Each step kicked up rain as it charged toward Ben. The Grey leapt into the air as Ben's sword raised to impale it. The creature dropped to the ground dead as Ben continued on his path. The storm raged as the three reached the prison. "You two wait here," Ben demanded. "If anyone else comes out, kill them," He ordered before entering alone.

Cj Callahan found an abandoned horse in the rain and managed to mount it. The four legged animal maneuvered through the mud while Cj fired arrows from its back. The pair worked together well despite his lack of experience riding. *The alien's must have trained you well,* He thought. The pair slowed to a stop as they reached a dead end street.

"Not that way," Cj called out to his steed. He pulled the animal's reins trying to get it to move. Out of nowhere an alien jumped onto him, pulling him to the ground. The two struggled in the rain as the alien got the advantage on the young man. The grey creature hammered its fists down on the defenseless Cj. One of the blows connected with his throat, choking him. As the alien continued to pummel Cj's body the horse nearby stomped its hooves. It kicked back its hind legs throwing the Grey off of Cj Callahan. The young man coughed as he rolled onto his stomach. He looked over at his assailant to see the blow had been fatal. "Oh yeah," Cj coughed, "This is definitely my horse now." As Cj limped over to his horse he heard a voice. He turned back to see a familiar figure nearby. Sarah Callahan stood in the rainy street of Paragon. She had returned with the aliens and looked as though she had not eaten in days. Her hair was ripped out of her head in several places, and she had a layer of dirt on her face. "Sarah!" Cj cried out to his sister. The teen girl recognized the name and rejected it. She opened her crusty lips and let out a horrific scream, imitating the aliens. Cj's horse bucked, causing him to look away from his sister. When Cj glanced back she was gone. A smile wiped across his face knowing that she was at least alive and out there somewhere. He vowed to keep looking for her as he mounted his horse again.

Ben Miller approached Scott's cell in the dark. The noise outside was dissipating as Ben leaned into the bars. "Scott," Ben called out in the dark. Behind him a noise came from Mr. Bolton's cell. "I don't think he wants to talk to you," Mr. Bolton laughed. Ben turned back to the prisoner. "Shut up," he fired off. He returned his attention to Scott's cell.

"You've always been a pain," Ben shouted into the dark. "Always coming into work high," Ben continued. "I kept these people alive all these years. Not you. You were busy joining the aliens." Ben leaned in. "Aren't you going to say anything?" Ben shouted. The cell in front of him remained quiet. "So many people have died because of you," Ben laughed. Out of the darkness of the cell a winged blade thrust forward. The force behind the weapon cut through the bars of the cell stabbing into Ben's chest. Ben coughed up blood as he looked down at the sword penetrating his suit. "They died because of you," Al scoffed as he stepped forward. He drove the blade deeper into Ben's wounded chest as he got closer. Ben struggled as Al drove the sword deeper, causing his lungs to fill with blood. "How else would a guy like you be carrying Landry's sword?" Al questioned to his victim in regards to the sword on his hip.

Daphne's front door burst open as four Grey's entered. Jason screamed from the couch. Daphne killed an attacker with the knife she had concealed earlier that day. One of the Grey's grabbed her as the other two went for Scott and Jason. Everything slowed down in Scott's head as he saw the scene play out. He did not want to hurt the Grey's but they were threatening his family. Without thinking Scott removed the sword Al had given him from its scabbard. He brought it down on the alien in front of him. The blade cracked the aliens skull as Scott turned to his son. The other Grey had not reached the boy. Scott ran into the middle of his son and the alien. The Grey tried reaching out with both hands for the child. Scott swept the metal blade up from the floor slicing the aliens limbs clean off. The appendages fell to the floor as Daphne stabbed the creature in the back. Scott looked back to see she had killed her second assailant with ease. The three of them embraced among the dead aliens.

Ben Miller's body was left alone in the prison. Al unlocked himself before freeing Mr. Bolton. Outside they found the dead bodies of two guards. Mr. Bolton collected a sword before they took to the streets to join the forces of Paragon. The remaining Grey's were overpowered as Al and the others killed the last of their warriors in the late hours of the night. Thunder boomed above as the city of Paragon cheered. They had survived the onslaught together.

Chapter Thirty-Three

Scott Carter woke up from his afternoon nap. The alterations made to Scott's body by the aliens did not stop Daphne from keeping him up late most nights. He stretched his arms out in his bed before getting up. There was a knock at his front door. He walked through the halls of his home tracing his fingertips along the wall. Daphne greeted him as he entered the front of their home. "Where's Jason?" Scott remarked. Daphne smiled at her man. His beard had grown long since returning to her. "He's in his room getting ready," Daphne said through her grin. The knock continued at their door. "We'd better answer that," She said with a wink.

Scott opened his front door and greeted Al and David Rodrigues. The two brothers entered the home as Cj Callahan and Mr. Bolton came up the path behind them. "Everyone's here," Daphne exclaimed. She was excited to see their guests.

Daphne had given up living within the walls of Paragon in favor of living with Scott. The three of them shared a home not far from the city. It had taken them months to make it livable and now everyone had gathered to celebrate.

"What's going on in the city?" Scott asked. Cj Callahan grinned as he looked to Mr. Bolton. "Well, we have excellent leadership now," Cj laughed. David and Al nodded along. Mr. Bolton smiled and waved his hand, "We have a lot of good people back home that voted for it," He replied. "It's a shame they don't know the truth about Scott," David cut in. Al nodded in favor of his brother's comment. "They will," Mr. Bolton promised. "Give them time and eventually you'll be welcomed into Paragon," Bolton assured Scott. Al pulled out a book. "Scott," Al spoke. Scott looked over to the book in Al's hand. Al looked over to his brother. "Our father was working on this, maybe you'd like to go through it?" David declared. Al extended the book out to Scott. He opened it to see the picture of himself that Tiago had taken.

"He was recording everything that happened after the aliens invaded," Al said with a sigh. Scott flipped through the book. "There's still some empty pages in here," Scott remarked. "Maybe you should keep the story going," Scott said as he handed the book back to Al.

After everyone shared a meal and plenty of laughter they said their goodbyes. Scott and Daphne cleaned up from the party before putting Jason to bed. Scott tucked his son in and kissed his forehead. "Goodnight, Dad," Jason whispered softly. Scott smiled as he looked back at the child in his bed, "Goodnight, son," he replied.

As they settled into bed for the night Scott kissed Daphne's forehead. "He called me Dad," Scott laughed as he talked. Daphne smiled back at him. "See, he just needs time," Daphne stated. Scott leaned back into his bed. "Still," He said, staring at the ceiling. "I wish we could find more to bond over. There's nothing to do here," Scott sighed. Daphne rested her head on Scott's grey chest. "What would you be doing if none of this ever happened?" Daphne asked. She smiled to herself as she thought of the answer to her own question. "Smoke," they both said at the same time. Scott laughed as Daphne sat up. "That reminds me," She said running to her closet. "What?" Scott shouted back. "Don't tell me you have weed," The excitement carried in his voice. Daphne shook her head while her back remained to Scott. "Not quite," She called back to him. Daphne fumbled with her belongings for a moment before returning to Scott. "I kept your things for as long as I could," she said holding out her hand. Scott reached out as she dropped something into his palm. "After awhile I had to let you go, but I kept that for a special occasion," Daphne said as she pointed to the seed in Scott's hand. "How's that?" She asked.

Scott rolled the striped seed around with his finger. He looked up to Daphne and replied, "I love you."